WHEN LION COULD FLY

WHEN LION COULD FLY

And other Tales from AFRICA

Told by Nick Greaves
Illustrated by Rod Clement

BARRON'S

Also by Nick Greaves,
When Hippo Was Hairy (Barrons, 1988)

First edition for the United States and Canada
published 1993 by Barron's Educational Series, Inc.

All inquiries should be addressed to:
Barron's Educational Series, Inc.
250 Wireless Boulevard
Hauppauge, New York 11788

Library of Congress Catalog Card No. 93-21841
International Standard Book No. 0-8120-6344-9 (hardcover)
                                            0-8120-1625-4 (paperback)

Library of Congress Cataloging-in-Publication Data

Greaves, Nick.
When lion could fly and other tales from Africa / told by Nick
Greaves; illustrated by Rod Clement.
144p.   22 x 17.2cm.
ISBN 0-8120-6344-9 (hardcover). — ISBN 0-8120-1625-4 (pbk.)
1. Tales — Africa. 2. Animals — Africa— Folklore. I. Clement,
Rod. II. Title.
GR350.G73 1993   93-21841
398.24'5'096—dc20   CIP
                                                AC

A David Bateman Book
Produced by David Bateman Ltd
32-34 View Road
Glenfield, Auckland 10
New Zealand

Design: Errol McLeary
Typeset by Typeset Graphics Ltd.
Printed in Hong Kong by Everbest Printing Co.
3456   987654321

Contents

Acknowledgments

A great many people helped in the preparation of this book—some knowingly, some unwittingly. For their advice and for additional information I am indebted to Dr. John Hutton, Dr. Don Broadley, and Mr. Hadebe, all formerly of the Natural History Museum of Zimbabwe. Mr. Ron Thomson, Mr. Ian Thomson, and the late Mrs. Babs Thomson, all formerly of the Zimbabwe Department of National Parks and Wildlife Management. Dr. Peter Mundy and Mr. Ivan Ncube of the Zimbabwe Department of National Parks and Wildlife Management. Dr. Rosalie Osbourne of the Kenya Wildlife Conservation and Management Department, Mr. Francis Odoom, and the Languages Institute of Ghana.

Special thanks are also due to the illustrator, Mr. Rod Clement, and to Allan Gardener of the World Wildlife Fund for Nature.

I am also most grateful to my wife Steph for helping to organize the typing of the first draft and to my son Douglas for being the guinea pig again.

Introduction

The teeming herds of Africa are now a fading memory and the African continent is facing a new and graver threat—overpopulation. The land is grazed bare. Each year, Africa loses more and more rainforest regions, wilderness areas and valuable farmlands, as the abused land turns to desert. The changes to the regional and global climate due to this ecological disaster mostly go unchecked.

Africa is at a turning point. We must make sure that the few isolated patches of wilderness remain intact for future generations. They are part of the complex web of life that has nurtured humankind and allowed us to become what we are today. Their potential loss is a threat to us and a threat to our planet's future.

This book complements *When Hippo Was Hairy*. It hopes to show that the rich heritage of African folklore involves the small creatures as well as the great and that we are all part of the great diversity of life that is now at stake.

It is hoped that some of you who read these and other similar books will care enough when it is your time to run things to bring this period of ignorance and greed to an end; to make amends with Mother Nature and to heal the wounds made by previous generations.

General Information

DISTRIBUTION (See maps)
These maps are a general guide to the distribution of the animals highlighted in this book. Nowadays, the animals may not occur throughout large tracts of their natural range due to the activities of people. This applies especially if the animal is considered a threat to or in competition with domesticated animals or crops. Many species used to range right down to the Cape of Good Hope in South Africa, but with the arrival of European settlers four centuries ago, years of hunting and persecution meant that very few large animals now occur outside of nature reserves.

It is interesting to compare the distribution of various animals with the vegetation zones of Africa. A lot of information about the habits and diet of different species can be gained from this simple exercise.

INFORMATION
The data on size, weight, lifespan, etc., are for an average-sized specimen. This information should help the reader to appreciate the differences in size and general lifestyles of the various animals.
Note: Heights are quoted at the shoulder and lengths include tails unless stated otherwise.

AFRICAN TRIBES
The African peoples referred to in these stories inhabit vastly different areas of sub-Saharan Africa. Although the climate, vegetation, religion, language, and customs may vary widely from, say, the Zulu of the Natal coast in the southeast, to the Pygmy of the central African rainforest, the stories are amazingly similar throughout much of the continent.

This similarity is partially explained by the fact that the Bantu peoples of Africa originated from a common ancestry in western central Africa. Over the past 2000 years, the Bantu people spread further and further across central, eastern, and southern Africa, conquering and assimilating the original inhabitants of these lands.

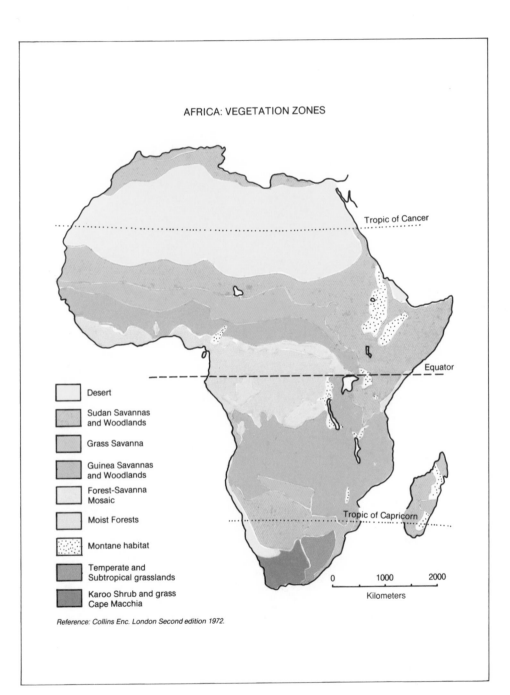

AFRICA: VEGETATION ZONES

Tropic of Cancer

Equator

Tropic of Capricorn

Desert

Sudan Savannas
and Woodlands

Grass Savanna

Guinea Savannas
and Woodlands

Forest-Savanna
Mosaic

Moist Forests

Montane habitat

Temperate and
Subtropical grasslands

Karoo Shrub and grass
Cape Macchia

0   1000   2000

Kilometers

Reference: Collins Enc. London Second edition 1972.

METRIC CONVERSIONS

For use in countries where the Metric system of measurement is used, the height, length, and weight conversions for the different animals in the Facts sections are:

	Height/Length*		Weight		Weight at Birth
	Male	Female	Male	Female	Male/Female
Serval	60cm	60cm	11kg	9kg	—250g—
Caracal	50cm	40cm	17kg	12kg	—400g—
Banded Mongoose	18cm	18cm	2kg	1.6kg	—20g—
Aardvark	60cm	53cm	55kg	50kg	—1.8kg—
Pangolin*	60cm	60cm	15kg	15kg	—300g—
Porcupine	30cm	30cm	18kg	18kg	—400g—
Vervet Monkey*	105cm	105cm	5.5kg	4.5kg	—350g—
Tree Squirrel*	35cm	35cm	200g	200g	—9g—
Greater Kudu	150cm	120cm	225kg	180kg	—16kg—
Bushbuck	90cm	70cm	50kg	36kg	—4kg—
Duiker	60cm	60cm	18kg	20kg	—1.5kg—
Vulture*	90cm	100cm	5kg	6kg	—140g—
Guinea Fowl*	60cm	53cm	1.8kg	1.2kg	—20g—
Honeyguide*	20cm	18cm	57g	50g	—5g—
Crocodile*	5m	4m	1000kg	800kg	—30cm*—
Python*	6m	6m	55kg	55kg	—60cm*—
Chameleon*	30cm	30cm	115g	115g	—7cm*—
Dung Beetle*	4cm	4cm	20g	20g	—

In the Beginning…

(A story told by the Fon Tribe of Dahomey in Central Africa)

When the Creator made the Earth he commanded a great snake to gather the material together with its huge coils. This gave the Earth its shape, so that people and all manner of birds and beasts could live upon it.

This Ancient Snake erected four pillars North, South, East, and West and his coils keep the pillars upright. These pillars hold up the heavens. The Ancient Snake has skins of black, white, and red that he puts on for night, daylight, and twilight.

In the beginning, Ancient Snake found only stagnant water on the Earth, so he shaped out courses for the streams and channels for the rivers and thus the world received life. And when Ancient Snake carried the Creator through the new world, mountains appeared wherever they stopped.

When the Creator finished his work, he saw there were too many mountains, trees, and large animals for the Earth to carry alone. So he asked Ancient Snake to coil himself up and to hold his tail in his mouth and so support the Earth. The Creator then told Red Colobus Monkey to feed Ancient Snake whenever he got hungry.

Today, the Ancient Snake still sustains the Earth. But every so often, Ancient Snake shifts his position to relieve an ache or an itch and in doing so creates earthquakes.

Should Red Colobus Monkey ever fail to feed Ancient Snake, the snake's hunger would force him to eat his own tail. If this ever happens, the Earth will slide into the ocean and that will be the end of our world.

(A story from the Pygmies in Central Africa tells us that when the Creator made the Earth the first animal to live upon it was Chameleon.)

Chameleon wandered far and wide in the first forest. But he was very sad for he was totally alone. One day, after a long, lonely time, Chameleon heard a strange whispering sound coming from a huge forest tree. The sound was like birds chirping or water running; however, Chameleon did not know what these sounded like and so he was curious to find the source of the noise.

Taking a sturdy log, Chameleon struck the trunk of the huge tree many times until at last water came out in a great flood that spread all over the Earth. With the water came all the birds, beasts, fishes, and insects that now dwell upon the Earth. Last of all, as the flood of water came to an end, a man and a woman appeared. They were the first Pygmies.

Serval and Tortoise

(A Tswana story)

Long, long ago Tortoise was slowly crawling home when he met Serval on his path.

"Hello old friend," said Serval heartily. "Have you found much to eat today?"

"No," replied Tortoise sadly. "Hardly anything at all."

Serval began to dance up and down and chortle with laughter. He had a mischievous idea. "Follow me, poor old Tortoise. And when you get to my home, I will have supper ready for you."

Tortoise gratefully accepted as Serval turned around and gaily bounced along the track that led to his home. Tortoise followed as fast as he could. But he was very slow, especially when he went uphill. Though he was tired, the thought of a lovely meal kept him going, so on he plodded.

When Tortoise eventually reached the patch of scrub Serval called home, Serval was laughing to himself. As soon as he caught sight of Tortoise, he teased him. "Goodness me, what a long time that took!"

"I'm sorry," apologized Tortoise as he regained his breath, "but surely you have had enough time to get the meal ready, so do not grumble."

"Oh, yes indeed!" replied Serval. "There is your meal," he chortled, pointing up to the branches overhanging his home. Poor Tortoise could only look wistfully at the distant meal, well out of his reach.

Serval was very pleased with his prank and ran off laughing. All Tortoise could do was slowly crawl off to his home hoping that tomorrow would bring a decent meal. He also began to plot his revenge.

Several weeks later, Tortoise sent Serval an invitation to eat with him. Serval was surprised; but knowing Tortoise to be a good-natured fellow, he

thought to himself, "Oh well, Tortoise must have seen the joke and bears me no malice. I'll go along and see what I can get out of him."

As it was the dry season, Tortoise had burned a patch of grassland near his home by the river. Serval had to cross this large patch of land to get to the savory smells wafting from Tortoise's home.

"Ah, my friend Serval," said Tortoise. "Look at the state of you! You are covered with black spots and your paws are filthy. Run back to the river and clean yourself up and then you can have supper. You really do have poor manners!"

Serval scampered off to the river to wash, as he was keen to taste the supper that smelled so good. On his return, he had to cross the burned ground again. He arrived just as dirty as before.

"That will never do! Off to the river with you and get properly cleaned up!" shouted Tortoise, with his mouth full of food.

Serval went back to the river time and time again, but try as he might, he was always dirty on his return. And each time Serval returned, Tortoise refused to serve him. Serval could see that the delicious food was disappearing fast.

As Tortoise gulped down the last morsel of food, Serval realized that he had been tricked. With a cry of embarrassment, he hurried across the burned ground for the last time and ran all the way home.

"That will teach you a lesson, my friend," said Tortoise, laughing the last laugh. Full and content, Tortoise withdrew into his shell for a good night's sleep.

To this day, Serval is still covered in black spots from the soot of the burned *vlei*.

How Serval Got His Spots

(A Ndebele fable)

In the beginning, Serval used to be the same tawny color as Lion, but he was much smaller and nowhere near as strong. The other animals often teased him, calling him "Lion's Little Cousin."

Serval dreamed of having a magnificent coat like Leopard or Zebra. If he could not be big and strong, he could at least be handsome.

One day, when Serval was going about his daily hunt, he met Puff Adder.

"Oh, kind Serval," pleaded Puff Adder, "I am feeling very ill and none of the other animals will help me."

"No wonder!" exclaimed Serval. "You are such a nasty creature that all animals go in fear of you. But because you are ill, I will help you just this once. But you must promise to keep your fangs to yourself!"

Puff Adder agreed willingly to be on his best behavior, so Serval took him home and looked after him. It took a long time for Puff Adder to get better as he was indeed very ill. Thanks mainly to Serval's care and attention, he eventually recovered.

Before Puff Adder left, he thanked Serval for his kindness. To show his gratitude, he said, "I will give you anything within my power in return for your kindness."

Serval replied, "There is nothing I would like more than a beautiful coat."

"That I can do," answered Puff Adder. "I will have to bite you, but do not fear that my poison will harm you. It will only be a very small amount."

So Puff Adder bit Serval carefully. Though it made Serval feel a bit sick, he quickly recovered. Soon his skin broke out in a rash and his tawny coat changed to a golden color mottled with black spots. Serval was overjoyed. He was now one of the most handsome creatures in the bush.

As a sign of respect for each other, Puff Adder and Serval do not trouble each other to this day.

FACTS ABOUT SERVALS
SPECIES:
SERVAL *(Felis serval)*
Nocturnal and usually solitary.

	Male	Female
Height	2 ft	2 ft
Weight	24¼ lb	20 lb
Weight at Birth	½ lb	½ lb
Age of Weaning	6 months	6 months
Age at Maturity	2 years	18 months
Gestation Period	—	72 days
Number of Young	—	2–4
Lifespan	12 years	12 years

Identification The serval is an elegant member of the cat family with a beautiful yellow coat with black spots and bars. It has long legs, a long neck, and large rounded ears on a smallish head. The tail is short, only about half the length of the head and body.

Habitat Servals are restricted in their range by their habitat requirements. They require a reliable source of water and are common in areas of higher rainfall. Servals also require stands of tall grass, underbrush, or reed beds in which they rest during the day.

Habits Although predominantly nocturnal, servals may be seen during the early morning and late afternoon. They are generally solitary, though mating pairs move and hunt together for a short while and youngsters will accompany their mothers for some considerable time.

Like most small carnivores, the serval has a small territory of about 2 square miles (5 sq km). It patrols this home range along established routes or trails. By leaving droppings along these trails, the serval marks its territory.

Unlike most members of the cat family, the serval will hunt in swampy areas where the water can be up to 3 inches (8 cm) deep.

Diet A serval's diet is made up of a wide range of prey. As they eat mainly rodent pests (up to 75 percent of their total diet), servals are the farmers' allies. But they will eat birds, reptiles, insects, amphibians, and scorpions as well.

Breeding The female has her young in the middle or latter part of the wet season, when cover is thickest. The litter of usually two or three kittens is born either in thick clumps of high grass or in thick scrub.

The young are born with a soft wooly coat much grayer than that of the adults. If she is disturbed, the female will carry her young off one by one to another secure hiding place. The young remain with the mother for many months after weaning.

Lion and Caracal

(A Batonka story)

One day, long ago, Lion was very thirsty after a long and difficult hunt. He wanted to go to drink at the river, but a large buffalo he had caught lay at the top of a high bank.

"Caracal, you must look after my buffalo while I go to drink at the river. Do not dare to eat any meat until I return and have my fill," ordered Lion.

"Very well, Uncle Lion," agreed Caracal.

Lion went down to the river, passing around the steep bank. As soon as he had gone, Caracal and his wife ate greedily from the buffalo.

On his return, Lion could not climb the steep bank. "Caracal, help me," he shouted.

"Yes, Uncle Lion. I will let down a rope so that you may pull yourself up." Caracal turned and whispered to his wife, "Give me one of the old thin ropes." Then aloud he added, "Wife, give me one of the strong buffalo hide ropes so Uncle Lion will not fall!"

Caracal's wife gave him an old, rotten rope. They continued to eat ravenously from the carcass while they let down the rope. Lion seized the rope and struggled up the steep bank. When Lion was near the top, Caracal gave the rope a jerk. The old rope broke and Lion tumbled all the way down the bank.

Caracal began to beat a dry hide. He howled and cried, "Wife, why did you give me a rope so bad it caused Uncle Lion to fall?"

Lion heard the commotion and roared, "Caracal, stop beating your wife. I will beat you if you do not stop! Help me climb up."

"Uncle Lion, I will give you a strong buffalo rope that will not break," Caracal shouted. Then he whispered to his wife, "Give me another old, thin rope."

Caracal let down the rope. Lion was nearly at the top of the bank when SNAP—the rope broke again and Lion fell down a second time. Once more Caracal began to beat the old hide, shouting, "Wife, did I not say to give me a strong rope?"

Lion roared, "Caracal, stop beating your wife at once. Help me instantly or you will regret it!"

"Wife," Caracal shouted aloud, "give me the strongest rope we have." Then he quietly said to her, "Give me the worst rope of all."

Caracal let down the third rope. But again as Lion was about to reach the top, Caracal gave a strong tug and once more the rope broke. Poor old Lion rolled down the hill a third time and lay bruised and stunned at the bottom of the bank.

Pretending to be concerned, Caracal inquired, "Uncle Lion, have you hurt yourself? Are you in much pain? Stay still, I am coming to help you."

But Caracal and his wife continued eating from the buffalo until they had had their fill. Then they slowly walked away.

Since that day, Caracal has lived a lonely, solitary life always in fear of his bigger, stronger relation.

Caracal, Eland, and Jackal

(A Bushman story)

Caracal was returning home from a hunting foray when he bumped into Eland. Caracal had never seen Eland before. Approaching warily, he said, "Good day friend! What may your name be?"

Eland struck the ground with his huge forefoot, raising a great cloud of dust. He replied in a deep, gruff voice, "I am Eland! Who are you?"

Caracal, in awe at the size of the King of all the antelopes, quietly answered, "I am Caracal." Then, in fear, Caracal ran home as fast as he could.

Jackal lived nearby and, when they met, he asked Caracal what was worrying him.

"Friend Jackal, I am quite out of breath and half dead with fright. I have just seen a fearsome looking fellow, with a large thick head and huge twisted horns. I asked him his name and he answered, 'I am Eland.'"

"What a foolish fellow you are to let such a lovely piece of flesh go untasted!" laughed Jackal. "Tomorrow we shall go to trap Eland and eat a huge feast together."

Next day, the two set off to look for Eland. But as they appeared over a hill, Eland saw them. He ran to his wife and said, "I fear that this is our last day, for Caracal and Jackal are coming to kill us. What shall we do?"

"Do not be afraid," said Eland's wife. "Take our child and make him cry as if he were hungry." Eland hesitated, but then he saw the reason for his wife's request. He did as she said, and went to meet Jackal and Caracal.

As soon as Caracal saw Eland, he was overcome with fear. Jackal was ready for this and he tied Caracal to himself with a leather thong. In this way, they would stand steadfast.

Eland prodded his calf with his horns. This made the youngster bleat and cry in surprise. Then Eland called out, "You have done well, friend Jackal. You have brought Caracal for us to eat. Hear how my youngster cries for food."

At these frightening words, Caracal was terrified. He pleaded with Jackal to untie him but Jackal was hungry and would not hear of it.

This was more than poor Caracal could stand. He set off at a tremendous pace to the safety of his house, dragging Jackal behind him. Caracal didn't stop. He pulled Jackal through bushes, over rocks, and through streams.

Eventually an exhausted Caracal reached home. Poor Jackal was scratched and bruised from his ordeal.

Eland had escaped and was never bothered by Caracal and Jackal again. And they are still in awe of this huge antelope to this day.

FACTS ABOUT CARACALS
SPECIES:
CARACAL *(Felis caracal)*
Solitary and nocturnal.

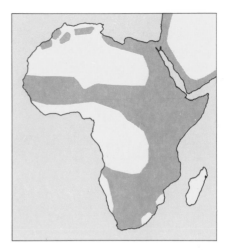

	Male	Female
Height	1½ ft	1¼ ft
Weight	38 lb	26 lb
Weight at Birth	14 oz	14 oz
Age at Weaning	6 months	6 months
Age at Maturity	18 months	18 months
Gestation Period	—	79 days
Number of Young	—	2–3
Lifespan	10 years	12 years

Identification A robust member of the cat family with a sandy brown to brick red coat and a paler throat and belly. The tail is notably shorter than any other African cat.

Habitat As the caracal can tolerate much drier conditions than the serval, it has a wider distribution. Open savannas with woodland, especially open *vleis* and grasslands with scattered clumps of acacia trees and high grasses are preferred. Caracals are not found in forested areas or above 5500 feet (1700 m) above sea level.

Habits Caracals are solitary creatures and being nocturnal are rarely seen by day. Although they generally prefer to stay on the ground, caracals are good climbers and have powerful claws to assist them.

The females have a territory of about 4½ square miles (12 sq km) and males a territory of up to 16 square miles (42 sq km). This allows a male's territory to overlap the territories of several females. Courtship and mating is a brief affair and both animals quickly return to their usual solitary habits.

Caracals are so well camouflaged and so good at concealing themselves, they are often overlooked. If disturbed, they quickly make off at high speed.

Diet Caracals are hunters and do not, as a rule, eat carrion. Their prey is small to medium size, including the young of antelopes, birds, small mammals, and even fish.

Breeding The female usually has a litter during the rainy season (September to December), though young can be born in the dry season as well. The female will seek dense cover in which to have her litter and she particularly likes abandoned aardvark holes.

There are usually two or three kittens and they are born blind. At ten days old they can see, and they become active soon after. The caracal's characteristic black ear tufts are noticeable by the time the kittens are two weeks old.

Why Mongoose Kills Snakes
(A Bushman legend)

In ancient times, Mongoose and Secretary Bird were great friends. One day they were walking through the bush when they came upon a large snake.

Snake asked Mongoose to accompany him. He had found something special and wished to show it to Mongoose. Secretary Bird said she was hot. She wished to bathe and drink at a water hole some distance away. So Secretary Bird said farewell to her friend Mongoose and flew off.

Mongoose and Snake set off together. After a long walk, they came to a nest on the ground. The nest had some eggs in it. Snake knew that the nest belonged to Secretary Bird, but he did not tell Mongoose this.

"Have you ever tasted eggs?" Snake asked Mongoose.

"No, Snake, I have never eaten an egg," replied Mongoose eagerly.

"They are very good. Why don't you try one?" suggested the cunning Snake. He broke open the shell of one of the eggs.

Both Mongoose and Snake started to eat the eggs. Mongoose agreed that he never knew anything that tasted so good. Just as they had gulped down the last egg, they saw Secretary Bird approaching.

The devious Snake called out, "Mongoose has eaten all your lovely eggs!"

Secretary Bird was very angry and very sad that her friend Mongoose had betrayed her. Then she saw that Snake had egg around his mouth too!

"You have *both* eaten my eggs," Secretary Bird said furiously.

Mongoose explained to Secretary Bird how Snake had tricked him. Then both Secretary Bird and Mongoose set upon the deceitful Snake and killed him.

"From now on, we shall both watch for snakes and kill them," said Mongoose to Secretary Bird—and they have done so ever since.

Secretary Bird learned how to build her nest atop thick, thorny trees to protect her eggs and young from predators. She also eats snakes; stamping them to death with her long legs and horny, scaled feet.

Mongoose eats snakes, too. He is able to kill them by being quicker than lightning and faster than even the speediest snake.

But Mongoose never forgot the lovely taste of the eggs and whenever he can find any he will always eat them.

Why Bat Flies at Night

(A Zulu story)

Once upon a time, Bat and Mongoose were great friends. All day long they would go hunting in the bush together. They would run between the trees and bushes and find good things to eat. When evening came, they would take turns cooking the meal and then eat it together.

But in spite of their apparent friendship, Bat did not like Mongoose—in fact he hated him. They were enjoying their supper one evening when Mongoose asked, "Why is your food always so much tastier than mine? Will you show me tomorrow how you make it, please?"

Bat agreed. But he had an evil plan forming in his mind. The next day Bat prepared the meal as usual. It was a delicious meal as Bat was a very good cook. Then he hid his pot and filled another with warm water. A few minutes later Mongoose appeared and greeted his friend. He was eager for his cooking lesson.

"Watch me," said the evil Bat. "You will see I always boil myself in the stewing pot just before mealtime. Because my flesh is so sweet, it flavors the meal."

Mongoose was amazed when Bat pulled out the pot of warm water and jumped in. Bat shouted, "See, this is the boiling soup!" Bat jumped out and when Mongoose was not watching, he swapped the pots and served his usual delicious meal.

Bat explained that he got the best result when he used his own pot. Mongoose was impressed and promised that tomorrow he would try cooking a delicious meal.

Next evening, Mongoose made a big fire. Soon he had the food boiling away merrily. Then, as Bat had showed him, Mongoose jumped into the soup. Of course, he was terribly burned and dreadfully sore.

Now Mongoose realized Bat's deceit. He set off in a towering rage to teach Bat a lesson he would never forget. Bat heard Mongoose approaching and slunk away into the night, afraid of Mongoose's wrath. Bat hid in a hollow tree and although Mongoose searched very hard he could not find him.

To this day Mongoose carries the singe marks from the boiling soup across

his fur. And Bat continues to hide from Mongoose. Only at night, when he is driven by hunger to search for food, does Bat come out. Never again could Bat cook his beautiful meals over a fire for fear of being discovered. And never again did Mongoose use a fire. He still remembers his painful burns.

FACTS ABOUT MONGOOSES
SPECIES:
BANDED MONGOOSE *(Nuncios mungo)*
Gregarious, living in packs of between 6 and 60 individuals.

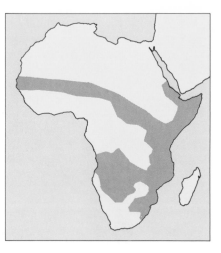

	Male	Female
Height	7 in	7 in
Weight	4½ lb	3½ lb
Weight at Birth	⅜ lb	⅜ lb
Age at Weaning	3–4 months	3–4 months
Age at Maturity	12 months	10 months
Gestation Period	—	60 days
Number of Young	—	2–8
Lifespan	5 years	5 years

Identification This small member of the mongoose family is distinguished by a coat that has a series of black bands across the body from the middle of the back to the base of the tail. The tail has a dark tip and is about half as long as the length of the body.

Habitat The banded mongoose will tolerate a wide range of habitats but does not live in desert areas or in dense forest. Vegetation rather than the presence of water seems vital, as is the presence of abandoned termite mounds, which it uses for dens.

Habits A gregarious animal, living in packs. Pack size can vary considerably and the largest ever recorded had 75 members.

The pack emerges with the warmth of the morning sun and starts foraging for food. When foraging, the pack scatters widely and members communicate by a continuous high-pitched twittering that can be heard some distance away.

A pack's territory covers approximately 11,000 square feet (1 sq km). The pack regularly marks stones, logs, or new objects in their territory with scent secreted from an anal gland. Within this territory, there will be temporary refuges the pack can retreat to when in danger. Also, if in serious danger, banded mongooses can climb trees and high termite mounds to survey the terrain.

When danger threatens, members of the pack give a shrill signal and the pack will freeze. Some individuals will stand on their back legs to view the surrounding area, using their tails as a balance. If danger is confirmed, the pack will slip silently away to the nearest refuge.

The pack uses abandoned aardvark holes, eroded gullies, and abandoned termite mounds as dens and often moves to new dens in their territory. A favorite den is regularly revisited.

Diet The banded mongoose eats insects, grubs, millipedes, snails, small rodents, small reptiles, scorpions, birds' eggs and nestlings, and fruit. Its acute sense of smell is used to locate subterranean insects and grubs that are quickly dug up. Old and sick members of the pack are looked after and provided with food by the others.

Breeding Several females within a pack come into heat at the same time. This benefits the pack because it limits the time it has to stay near the nursery den.

The litters of young are usually born in grass-lined nursery chambers within the den. The young are blind and nearly hairless at birth but within two weeks they can see and are active. Any of the females producing milk will feed the young. When the pack is off foraging, an adult will remain with the young at all times, though the mothers do not stray far from the den.

The pack will help to defend the young and move the young to a new den should danger threaten.

Why Aardvark Lives Underground

(A Shona story)

When the world was still young, Aardvark lived aboveground like all the other animals. Aardvark was a kindly, helpful creature and was a friend to all the animals of the bush.

One day Aardvark was roaming around his territory when he came across a young bird that had fallen from its nest and died. This upset Aardvark greatly for he knew the sorrow it would cause the young bird's parents.

As he walked on, he came across some beautiful butterflies that had died of thirst alongside a dry puddle. This sad sight made him even more upset for he loved to watch these colorful insects flutter among the flowers and shrubs.

Then Aardvark came across Baboon who had killed some birds and was taking them home to eat.

"I loved to watch those beautiful creatures. Now, alas, they will never sing or soar in the skies again!" Aardvark could not contain his grief. He burst into tears, full of sorrow at the harshness that existed in what could be a paradise for all.

As Aardvark traveled he saw more and more sad sights and heard even more tales of woe and disaster. Being so kindhearted, he could no longer bear the sorrow.

"I shall live underground in the future. I cannot bear to see more sad sights or meet anyone who will tell me of other sad happenings!"

True to his word, Aardvark dug a large burrow in the earth with his powerful front legs and he has lived in his tunnels ever since. Only at night, when most other animals are asleep, will Aardvark come out to search for food.

The Kindly Aardvark

(A Kikuyu story)

Long, long ago in the very beginning, Warthog possessed enormous ivory tusks and Elephant had only a small pair of tusks. This made Elephant very envious. He believed that the Creator should have bestowed such magnificent ornaments on him, the largest and most powerful animal in the bush.

Warthog's tusks were so huge that they trailed along the ground and weighed him down. Warthog would never admit it, but they could be a nuisance at times. However, he was tremendously proud of them.

Warthog's best friend was Aardvark. They lived close to each other and Aardvark had many burrows in Warthog's territory. Warthog and Aardvark spent many happy hours together.

One day Elephant sent an invitation to Warthog to visit him. As Warthog trotted off, Aardvark became worried as she knew Elephant was jealous of Warthog's tusks.

"You had better keep your wits about you. Don't trust Elephant, he will trick you in some way. My advice is to be on your guard!" Aardvark warned.

"Oh I will, Aardvark, I will! Thank you for your concern and advice," replied Warthog gratefully. "Will you be here long?"

"I have so many burrows that I do not need to stay long in one place. But I will stay here a few days longer. Should you need my help, I will be here," answered Aardvark.

Warthog found Elephant and while they were eating they had a long chat. Elephant breakfasted from the branches and Warthog dug up grass roots and tubers. Warthog was most flattered by Elephant's friendliness and when Elephant started to compliment Warthog on his magnificent tusks, he thought how kind and charming Elephant was. Warthog had forgotten Aardvark's warning.

"Warthog, your tusks are wonderful! I do believe they are the finest tusks in all Africa," said Elephant warmly. Warthog was blushing with pleasure at such compliments. "I wonder if... but no, I could not ask such a favor of you."

"What is it you want, friend Elephant?" asked Warthog, who was now totally off guard thanks to Elephant's cunning.

"Could I please try your tusks? Just to see how I would look with such fine ornaments. I promise I will return them promptly."

Warthog was only too pleased to help his new friend and so pulled out his great tusks. Elephant hurriedly removed his small tusks and put the big ones in place. Elephant looked at his reflection in a nearby pool and was very impressed by his splendid appearance.

"Yes, these will do very nicely," gloated Elephant. Then he wickedly beat poor, trusting Warthog and walked off with his new prize, saying, "You will never get these tusks back. They are mine now—mine, Mine, MINE!"

Poor Warthog used Elephant's small tusks to replace his magnificent stolen tusks. He knew that he looked ridiculous. And, to make matters worse, as he started to walk dejectedly home a heavy rain started to fall. It was a crestfallen Warthog that met Aardvark when he returned home at last.

"I forgot your warning about Elephant. What a fool I am," sobbed Warthog miserably. "Now Elephant has my beautiful tusks and I only have his little ones."

Aardvark became more and more indignant as she listened to Warthog's lament. "Poor Warthog," she said. "It is a shame and Elephant will be punished for his deceit. He shall never have a real home and he shall be hunted all the time for his ivory tusks. But you, Warthog, shall be safe and you shall shelter in a burrow for the rest of your days."

Warthog was incredulous. "But how can I shelter in a burrow? I cannot dig," he said.

"You shall use my burrows. I have so many and I am always digging new

ones. There are more than enough for both of us."

Since that day, generations of warthogs have lived safe from predators and bad weather in the burrows of aardvarks. All thanks to the kindness of Aardvark.

FACTS ABOUT AARDVARKS
SPECIES:
AFRICAN AARDVARK *(Orycteropus afer)*
Also known as the antbear. Solitary and nocturnal.

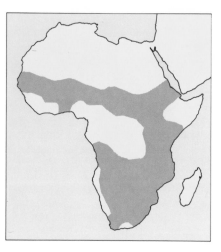

	Male	Female
Height	2 ft	1¾ ft
Weight	120 lb	115 lb
Weight at Birth	4 lb	4 lb
Age at Weaning	4 months	4 months
Age at Maturity	2 years	2 years
Gestation Period	—	7 months
Number of Young	—	1
Lifespan	10 years	10 years

Identification Aardvarks are unique among Africa's mammals. They have a superficial resemblance to pigs, with a long muzzle and ears and pale yellowish-gray, sparsely haired bodies. But here any resemblance ends. In profile, the body is arched and the highest point is the lower back as the back legs are much larger and heavier than the front legs. The aardvark has a thick, tapering tail and heavy, powerful legs with large claws adapted for digging.

Habitat The aardvark prefers woodland, scrub, and grassland, especially with sandy soils. They avoid areas prone to seasonal flooding. Aardvarks are not common but do live over a wide area.

Habits Solitary and almost entirely nocturnal, aardvarks seldom move about before 9 PM. But during the night they can cover several miles while foraging for food.

When foraging, they move slowly, with their noses close to the ground, snuffling out prey. They have poor eyesight but an excellent sense of smell and acute hearing. They can run off with surprising speed if disturbed.

Aardvarks dig shallow temporary burrows that may be used for one or two nights, but they also have more permanent and extensive burrows with numerous chambers and several entrances. These burrows are scattered around their territories, which are generally about 2 square miles (5 sq km) in size. Old burrows are important as homes and breeding dens to many of Africa's animals.

Diet The aardvark's diet of ants and termites is located by smelling out their nests. It then digs up the nest, and eggs, pupae, and adults are lapped up with the aardvark's long, sticky tongue.

Breeding A single youngster is born during the winter months of about May to August. Blind and hairless at birth, the young aardvark is born in a maternity den where it remains alone, the female returning from time to time to nurse it.

After two to three months, the youngster may accompany the mother on her nightly forays and at six months old, the youngster can dig for itself. It is not known how long the young remain with the mother, but they are not fully mature until two years old.

Why Pangolin Has Scales

(A story from the Angoni)

Long ago, Pangolin had a luxuriant coat of fur. Not only was his coat beautiful, it also protected him, for in ancient times Pangolin was a fearless robber of beehives.

Pangolin's rival was Honey Badger. To get to the honey he loved, Honey Badger had to back into the entrance of a beehive and emit a ghastly smell to make the bees drowsy. But this and his thick, tough skin did not prevent him from being stung sometimes.

However, Pangolin, with his beautiful protective coat, was unstoppable at robbing the bees of their precious honey. Finally, the bees pleaded with the Creator for some form of protection from the merciless attacks of Pangolin and Honey Badger.

As they were both so good at stealing honey, the Creator decided to see who was the most cunning of the two in obtaining honey. The winner would retain the privilege. Pangolin and Honey Badger set about their tasks with gusto as each was intent on winning the honor and their favorite meal for all time.

Pangolin was the most skillful. With his long, strong front legs and sharp claws, he quickly opened the hives. His long tongue lapped up the honey and he did the least damage to the hive.

Honey Badger on the other hand made quite a mess as he ripped the hives apart in his haste to get at the contents. Honey Badger also had help from Honeyguide, a bird who often helped Honey Badger to find the hives for a reward of delicious honey.

The competition was very close as the time for the Creator's decision drew near. Honey Badger feared he might lose and this worried him a great deal. One day, he was robbing a particularly large hive and getting stung more than usual when he realized that Pangolin's greatest asset was his thick fur coat. So Honey Badger thought of a scheme to beat Pangolin by unfair means.

One night, Honey Badger crept up to his sleeping adversary and poured honey all over him. Pangolin was sleeping so soundly he did not wake up. Then Honey Badger dripped a thin trail of honey to a nest of fierce red ants nearby. The ants loved nothing more than eating honey.

Pangolin was suddenly awakened by the painful bites of thousands of fierce red ants gathering the honey from his body. Though his fur protected him from bees, it was no match for the ants. Soon Pangolin was in agony. He was desperate to rid himself of these fiery biters.

In his desperation Pangolin rolled in the embers from a nearby bush fire. This drastic measure defeated the worrisome ants, but in the process Pangolin burned off his lovely coat. His pink skin was sore and swollen.

When Pangolin had recovered from his ordeal, he could not get near a beehive without getting badly stung. Pangolin had lost his protection!

Reluctantly, the Creator granted the victory and the spoils to Honey Badger. But he scolded him for winning more by deceit than cunning. The Creator took pity on Pangolin and promised that his protection would grow back. He said that Pangolin would be able to eat ants and termites instead of honey to make up for his loss.

Since that day, Honey Badger continues to raid beehives, though sometimes he still gets stung for his efforts. Pangolin, on the other hand, grew a special coat of horny, overlapping scales. These scales protect him from the fiercest ants and termites and Pangolin even grew to enjoy eating them!

FACTS ABOUT PANGOLINS
SPECIES:
CAPE PANGOLIN *(Manis temmincki)*
Also known as the scaly anteater. Nocturnal and solitary.

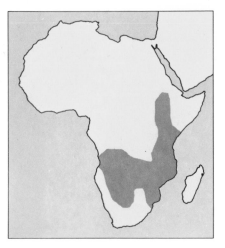

	Male	Female
Length	2 ft	2 ft
Weight	33 lb	33 lb
Weight at Birth	11 oz	11 oz
Age at Weaning	3 months	3 months
Age at Maturity	Not known	Not known
Gestation Period	—	Not known
Number of Young	—	1
Lifespan	Not known	Not known

Identification The pangolin is unmistakable as it is covered with an armor of heavy, brown scales. The head and limbs are covered with small scales and the body and tail have much larger, thicker, and heavier scales. The underparts and sides of the face are covered with dark skin that is tough and pliable.

Habitat The Cape pangolin lives in dry bush and savanna and prefers sandy soils. During the day, it rests in aardvark holes, hollow logs, or rock crevices.

As they are not dependent on a regular water supply, pangolins can survive in very dry areas with only seasonal water.

Habits They are solitary foragers and, although mostly nocturnal, they may occasionally be seen during daylight hours.

Pangolins move very slowly, often walking on their back legs using their tail to balance rather than using their clawed small front legs. Cape pangolins can climb over logs and other obstructions. If threatened, pangolins roll up into a tight ball, using their scales to protect the face and underside.

A pangolin's territory is around 3 square miles (8 sq km). Individuals will range over a small area within this territory for a month or two, and then they move to a new section. Pangolins mark their territory with a heavy, foul-smelling odor secreted from their anal glands.

Diet Pangolins eat mostly ants and termites. They locate the nests by smell and rip them open with their powerful clawed forelegs. They have a very long, sticky tongue that is inserted into the tunnels of the nest and withdrawn covered with eggs, larvae, and adults. In the process of eating, pangolins swallow a lot of soil and sand. This soil grinds up their food and helps them digest it, as they have no teeth to do so.

Breeding The pangolin gives birth during the cold, drier months of the year and only one youngster is produced. At birth, the scales are soft but they harden by the second day. The youngster clings to its mother's back with a vise-like grip. Its long front claws clamp under the female's back scales and its tail is clasped tightly across the mother's tail.

When very young, the infant will take refuge under the female, who will curl around it. As it grows and becomes too large to be completely enclosed, the female covers its head and shoulders while the youngster's tail is clasped across the mother's body. In this way, both mother and young protect their heads and undersides.

Why Porcupine Has Quills

(A Batonka story)

Long ago, Porcupine was a most handsome creature and he possessed a luxuriant coat of fur. As he looked so splendid, and many of the other animals often complimented him, Porcupine became quite vain.

One day, while Porcupine was talking to Jackal, he boasted that if all the animals were as beautiful as he, then the world would be an altogether much nicer place. This vain remark annoyed Jackal and so he plotted to spoil Porcupine's beauty once and for all.

Several days later, Porcupine happened to meet Jackal again. "Listen, Porcupine," said Jackal, pretending to be kind. "In that thorn thicket beyond the waterhole lives a *nganga* with powerful medicines that can make you look even more beautiful than you do now. Go over and seek his help. But leave your handsome coat of fur with me so that it will not get spoiled."

The conceited Porcupine fell for Jackal's clever ploy. He took off his much-admired coat and left it in Jackal's care. After thanking Jackal for his thoughtfulness, Porcupine started to make his way toward the patch of thorns.

Silly Porcupine reached the thorny patch and had only pushed himself in a short distance before he was badly pricked all over by the huge spikes. Try as he might, he could move no further forward. He had to haul himself out

backwards. This was very painful, for most of the thorns broke off and he could not pull them out.

"Aha," laughed the cunning Jackal. "As you could never get your lovely coat over all those ugly spines, I shall wear it myself!" And off Jackal ran, laughing all the way.

Today we see that Jackal wears a handsome coat of thick fur, whereas the dim-witted Porcupine hides away during the day. He only comes out after dark because all the other animals always mock him, remembering how boastful Porcupine was about his good looks.

FACTS ABOUT PORCUPINES
SPECIES:
CAPE PORCUPINE *(Hystrix africaeaustralis)*
Lives in pairs.

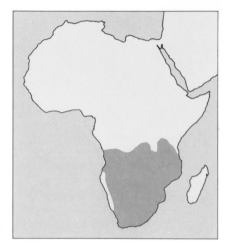

	Male	Female
Height	1 ft	1 ft
Weight	40 lb	40 lb
Weight at Birth	14 oz	14 oz
Age at Weaning	1 month	1 month
Age at Maturity	2 years	2 years
Gestation Period	—	7–8 weeks
Number of Young	—	1–3
Lifespan	8–20 years	8–20 years

Identification Porcupines are the largest rodents in sub-Saharan Africa. Their bodies are armed with long, flexible black and white spines and stout, sharp quills. The spines and quills cover the back, hindquarters, and the short, stubby tail. The spines are up to 20 inches (50 cm) in length and the quills up to 12 inches (30 cm). The remainder of the body is covered with a coarse coat of black hair and on each side of the neck there are white patches.

Habitat Porcupines are widely distributed from sea level up to altitudes of 6500 feet (2000 m). They are not found in forested areas and have a marked preference for rocky, hilly outcrops called *kopjes.*

Habits Porcupines live in pairs or sometimes in extended family groups. Active at night, porcupines use crevices, caves, and old aardvark holes for shelter during the day. They often modify these holes to suit their requirements by excavating with their front claws. If necessary, they can dig their own burrows.

The group often splits up to search for food at night. They are noisy animals and make a lot of snuffling and grunting as they forage. They are also noisy eaters.

Porcupines have acute hearing and, if disturbed, they stand motionless and are easily approached. However, porcupines can become aggressive, stamping their back feet and grunting. They can erect their quills at will, making themselves look twice as large. They also rattle the quills as a further warning. If they feel threatened, they defend themselves by running backwards or sideways at their tormentors. The quills are very sharp and can become deeply embedded in an enemy's body, inflicting painful and sometimes fatal wounds. This enables the porcupine to protect itself from animals as large as lions and leopards.

Diet The porcupines' diet is mostly vegetarian and includes bulbs, tubers, and roots that they dig up. Porcupines are also fond of fallen fruits such as wild fig, mobola plum, and the fruit of the sausage tree. They will often gnaw tree bark and can kill smaller trees. Porcupines also have a peculiar habit of gnawing bones and even old elephant ivory. They often take these bones back to the family den to chew on at their leisure.

Porcupines have benefited from agricultural development and can be a problem in some vegetable growing areas. Although they only eat some of the crop, they damage much of it.

Breeding Porcupines mate for life and the young are born during the summer months. The female has one litter a year of one to three young. The young are well-developed at birth and their eyes are already open. The body is covered with short, soft spines that harden and grow quickly.

The young start to forage and eat solid foods with their parents after the first month. The young remain with their parents until they are about sixteen months old. They then seek mates and territories of their own. Both male and female are involved in caring for the young.

Monkey's Heart

(A story from the Swahili of East Africa)

Long ago, at the edge of the ocean, there grew a huge tree that spread half its branches over the land and half over the sea. It was the favorite tree of Vervet Monkey. He would swing and play in its branches all day, stopping only to eat some of the tree's delicious fruit when he grew hungry.

In the sea lived a huge Tiger Shark. One day, Monkey threw a fruit into the water and Shark gobbled it up. As the fruit was so tasty, Shark swam close to the tree each morning. He made friends with Monkey and persuaded him to throw fruit for him to eat.

"Thank you, friend Monkey," said the grateful Shark. "I get so tired of eating fish all the time and the fruit is so delicious."

Monkey enjoyed Shark's friendship and he also enjoyed throwing fruit into the sea for Shark to gobble up.

As Monkey was swinging through the branches one day, Shark said, "You have been very kind to me these past months, providing me with delicious fruit each day. I would like to repay your kindness so I have decided to show you my home."

Monkey was wary of Shark's offer and replied, "I do not think I want to go, thank you. I do not swim well and I am not fond of getting my fur wet. I am much happier in my tree where I belong."

Shark pleaded with Monkey and Monkey became curious to see Shark's home. The great tree had nearly finished fruiting for the season and Monkey wondered if Shark would have some nice food to eat.

Eventually, Monkey agreed to accompany Shark to his home. Shark promised to let Monkey ride on his back so that Monkey would be safe and dry. Monkey jumped on to Shark's back and Shark swam off carefully. At first, Monkey was scared, but he soon got used to the movement and the strange sensations of the sea.

After some time, Monkey asked, "How much further to go?" He was getting impatient.

"We are about halfway there," answered Shark. "But there is something I must tell you first. The chief of our tribe, the biggest and most powerful Shark in the ocean, is very ill. We fear he may die. Our tribe's *nganga* has told us that the chief can only be cured by eating a monkey's heart. But because you have always been kind to me, I thought I would prepare you for the sacrifice which lies ahead."

Monkey was terrified. He bit his lip to stop crying out in fear while he planned his escape. At last, he said as calmly as he could, "My dear friend, how foolish of you not to have told me before we left the great tree. How can your chief have my heart when I did not bring it with me? Obviously you do not know much about monkeys. We leave our hearts hanging in the tree where we sleep."

Shark was very surprised by Monkey's statement. He knew how angry the rest of his tribe would be if what Monkey said was true.

Monkey easily persuaded Shark to return to the great tree so that they could take Monkey's heart to the chief of all sharks. As Shark swam back towards the great tree, he said, "If I take you back to your tree will you return with your heart?"

"Of course," replied Monkey. "Come, make haste so that we do not keep your chief waiting."

When Shark reached the great tree, Monkey quickly disappeared into the branches and did not return. Shark, who was now getting impatient to return

to his chief, called out, "Monkey! Monkey! Have you got your heart yet? How much longer must I wait?"

His reply was a half-rotten fruit that landed with a thud on his nose. A burst of laughter came from the foliage of the great tree. "What sort of fool do you think I am?" screamed Monkey. "Did you expect me to come back to be killed?"

"But you promised you would find your heart. Can you not find it?"

"Foolish fish!" laughed Monkey louder than ever. "My heart is here in the center of my body where it has always been! Now away with you! Our friendship is ended. You may find some other monkey stupid enough to go with you, but you will not get me!"

Monkey laughed and chattered in the great tree, pleased with his quick wits. Proudly he told all his friends and relations how he had outwitted the huge Tiger Shark.

Why Monkeys Look Like People

(A Shona fable)

Many years ago, a terrible famine struck the land and for a very long time no rain fell. As a result, no crops could be grown. The people who lived during those terrible times had little food to eat.

At last, the village elders decreed that all the remaining food would be stored in one safe place where it could be guarded from thieves and animals. The men chosen to guard the food were all proven warriors and were trusted not to steal it.

Time passed and the drought did not break. The food was in very short supply and the small daily ration left everyone hungry. Eventually, their hunger and the temptation of the food proved too much for one group of warriors. They started to eat. The next guards to come on duty found the thieves still eating and the angry warriors dragged the shamed men before the village council to be tried.

The village chief said to them, "You all look fit and strong. This is because you have been eating the food you were entrusted to guard. However, we will not kill you for this shameful act. But we will give you a lesson that you will not forget. You will be turned into animals that look almost human. People will drive you away from their homes because you will always be ready to steal. You will lurk in the cold trees in winter while we have warm fires. You will never live with us again!"

Then the powerful village *nganga* turned the thieves into the first monkeys. When they saw how they looked, they ran away to hide in the bush.

That is why today, when we watch a troop of Vervet Monkeys, they seem almost human, especially in the way mothers look after their babies and scold naughty youngsters.

FACTS ABOUT VERVET MONKEYS
SPECIES:
VERVET MONKEY *(Ceropithecus aethiops)*
Gregarious, living in troops of up to 20.

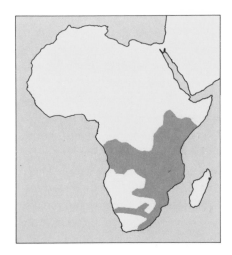

	Male	Female
Length	3½ ft	3½ ft
Weight	12 lb	10 lb
Weight at Birth	12 oz	12 oz
Age at Weaning	2 months	2 months
Age at Maturity	2 years	2 years
Gestation Period	—	175 days
Number of Young	—	1
Lifespan	10 years	10 years

Identification The vervet monkey is a grizzled, grayish color on its upper body with a yellowish tinge, whereas the underparts are a whitish color. The face is covered with short black hair with a white band across the forehead and down toward the chin. The tail is a gray color and darkens towards the tip. The soles of the hands and feet have bare, black skin.

Habitat Vervet monkeys live in woodlands and savannas, the fringes of forests, and high bush. They are not found in rainforests or semi-desert regions. During the wet season they will roam into more open grasslands in search of food.

Habits The vervet monkey lives in groups, or troops, of six to twenty individuals. Each individual in the troop has a clearly defined rank—both among the males, who are not related, and the females, who are related. This hierarchy is usually maintained with threats and visual warnings. Noisy fights do occur, however, especially when young males join the troop during the mating season.

The members of the troop spend a great deal of time grooming each other, which helps to strengthen group bonds and establish dominance—the more dominant animals receive more attention than lower-ranking individuals. Grooming also helps control pests such as fleas and ticks and cleans off dry skin.

The group scatters widely during the day to feed, but they regroup in the evenings, sleeping high up in trees or in rocky shelters.

Vervet monkeys communicate with each other using a wide range of calls. Scientists have discovered that the alarm call warning for a leopard is different to that of an eagle. This allows the monkeys to respond differently depending on whether the threat is on the ground or in the air.

When the males reach maturity, they leave the family troop and find a new troop to live with. Adult males may change troops several times during their lives.

Diet Predominantly vegetarian, vervet monkeys eat wild fruits, flowers, leaves, seeds, and seed pods. They have been known to eat birds' eggs and chicks, as well as insects and termites.

In farming areas the vervet monkey can become a problem, raiding vegetable crops, fruit plantations, and grain crops.

Breeding The young can be born any time of the year. When an infant is born, all the members take an interest in the youngster and its presence seems to strengthen the bonds within the troop. The mother cares for the youngster for the first two months of its life. It is then ready to become more independent and starts feeding for itself, learning what is good to eat from the mother.

The very young infant seldom strays far and clings tightly to its mother's chest and belly as she moves around. As the youngster becomes more independent, it will hitch rides on its mother's back. It is very playful at this age.

The males seem to watch out and care for their own youngsters, being quick to sound out should danger threaten.

What Squirrel Saw

(A story from the Hambakushu)

One very hot day long ago, a small Grass Snake was looking for a comfortable place to rest. Finding some long, soft grass beneath a shady tree, Grass Snake curled up and fell asleep.

Squirrel lived in this shady tree and, as he foraged along the branches, his sharp eyes noticed the sun shining on Grass Snake's skin. Squirrel began to chatter and mutter in alarm, attracting the attention of Lion.

"Hello," said Lion to himself. "I wonder why Squirrel is making all that noise?" Cautiously, Lion crept to the foot of the tree, and there he saw Grass Snake curled up in the long grass.

"So this is what all the noise is about!" Lion exclaimed with a hint of disappointment. "A mere grass snake is neither harmful nor good to eat!" And leaving Grass Snake asleep beneath the tree, Lion went on his way.

Not long after, Leopard came along the trail and she too heard Squirrel chattering.

"I'll just have a look to see what Squirrel is making such a fuss about," Leopard said to herself. Slowly, she crawled to the foot of the tree.

As soon as she saw Grass Snake, Leopard exclaimed in disgust, "I would not be thanked if I brought this home for supper. And as it is harmless, I will not waste my energy on it." Leopard turned back to the trail and continued her journey.

Squirrel kept up his chattering and along came Mongoose.

"What is that I hear?" Mongoose asked himself. "Squirrel does not make all this noise unless he has seen something interesting. Perhaps I shall find some supper if I follow his call."

Silently Mongoose crept to the foot of the tree. Seeing Grass Snake there, he pounced and devoured him all up.

"Thank you, little Squirrel!" called Mongoose, licking his lips. "I should not have known that the snake was here if you had not told me." And Mongoose went happily on his way.

Squirrel, who had watched all these proceedings from the safety of his tree, laughed to himself. "Now I realize that when you are safe from one creature, you are not always safe from another. I must take care not to make the same mistake myself!"

Then Squirrel leapt into the branches of a nearby tree and scampered around looking for a meal.

Squirrel and Spider's Web

(A Bushman story)

Long ago, all the animals were lonely for they had no mates. One day, they all gathered together to discuss how they could find mates to keep them company. Squirrel had thought carefully about their problem and had come up with an idea.

"I have heard that up in the sky beyond the clouds there are mates for all," Squirrel said.

"But how do we get there?" asked the other animals.

"I will spin a strong web and fasten it onto a cloud," said Spider. "Then you will be able to climb up the web and find mates." The animals agreed that this was a good plan.

So Spider began to spin the web and very soon even the animals with the keenest of eyes lost sight of him. Only a ladder of silver thread showed them where Spider had gone. Presently, Squirrel declared that everything was ready and he began to climb into the sky. All the other animals followed.

Despite the great weight of all the creatures and the trembling of the silken silver thread as Elephant, Lion, Buffalo, Baboon, and all the others began to climb, the web held fast. Everyone climbed higher and higher. Squirrel often turned back to urge them on.

At last, they reached the country above the clouds, and each found a mate there. Squirrel had been true to his word and all were happy as the formal arrangements for paying a dowry were finalized.

But it was not so with Squirrel. Although he had chosen a mate, he had made some excuse to her mother and father and had not paid his dowry. Instead, he had crept off and found a huge pile of millet corn to eat. Squirrel was famished and soon the huge pile was much smaller. Squirrel's appetite surprised even himself.

Then Squirrel began to worry what would happen to him when the theft was discovered. So he took some millet and chaff, and while Spider was busy talking to his new relatives, he rubbed the millet onto Spider by pretending to brush off some dust.

Soon after, the theft was discovered. The owner accused the animals of stealing his millet. Naturally, the animals proclaimed their innocence.

Cunning Squirrel stood up and said, "There is only one way of finding out who stole the millet. Let us search every animal and look for signs of millet seed and chaff. Some of it is bound to have clung to the fur of the culprit!" Squirrel had, of course, cleaned himself thoroughly.

And so the search began. Suddenly, Squirrel cried, "Oh no! Not you, Spider! How could you have done such a thing? You have millet clinging to your body. You must be the thief! Do not try to deny it!"

Despite Spider's pleas of innocence, all the other animals were very angry and they wanted to know why Spider had done such a deceitful thing.

Spider ran to his web. "I got you all up here, but you can get yourselves down again," he called out in disgust. Then Spider began to descend to Earth, rolling up his web as he went.

Now the animals were in a fix. Their ladder had gone and it was a long, long way down to Earth.

"Now what shall we do?" they asked one another. They had no desire to remain above the clouds for the rest of their lives.

"I am going to jump," said Baboon. And true to his word, he did so.

"So shall I," exclaimed Cheetah and he bounded after Baboon.

"That's right! That's splendid!" Squirrel said, as animal after animal leapt from the clouds. Squirrel did not tell them that they were jumping to their deaths.

Squirrel told Elephant to wait till last because he was so huge and cumbersome that he might fall on and hurt some of the smaller creatures. Eventually, when every other animal had gone, Squirrel told Elephant that it was all clear below and that now he could safely jump too.

"I'll come with you," said Squirrel. He leapt onto Elephant's back and clung on tightly as Elephant jumped toward the Earth. Poor Elephant landed with such a crash that he was killed instantly, but his huge body saved Squirrel from hitting the ground. Squirrel was not injured at all and he quickly ran off into the bush.

Since that day, no one has ever been able to climb up into the land above the clouds and those who have heard this tale have no wish to try.

The relatives of the animals who went to this land are suspicious of Squirrel even today, and they wonder how he was the only animal to survive. Perhaps that is why he spends so much time cleaning his fur—to make sure that there is no trace of millet left on him.

FACTS ABOUT TREE SQUIRRELS SPECIES:

TREE SQUIRREL (*Paraxerus cepapi*)

Solitary or found in small family groups.

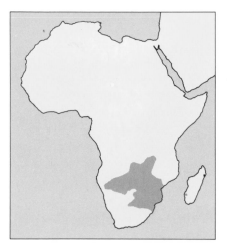

	Male	Female
Length	14 in	14 in
Weight	7 oz	7 oz
Weight at Birth	⅓ oz	⅓ oz
Age at Weaning	5 weeks	5 weeks
Age at Maturity	10 months	10 months
Gestation Period	—	55 days
Number of Young	—	1–3
Lifespan	6 years	6 years

Identification The tree squirrel can vary greatly in color and size. The color ranges from an overall grayish tone to a more rusty color. Usually, the lower parts of the body are lighter. The hairs on the body are coarse and the hairy tail is as long as the body. Dark whiskers on the face are conspicuous and the feet are equipped with short, sharp claws.

Habitat Common in open woodland, preferring acacia woodland where tree holes are more abundant. They avoid grasslands and dense forests.

Habits The tree squirrel is often solitary or found in small family units. Often, immature squirrels remain with the parents and help to raise the next litter of young.

Tree squirrels recognize each other by smell, identifying family members by sniffing nose to nose. They are highly territorial and will chase off intruders.

Although tree squirrels live in the trees, generally they search for food on the ground, so they must remain very alert. When alarmed, members of the family group will flick their tails with rapid, jerking movements and make loud clicking and "chucking" calls. If danger threatens, they run to the nearest tree. If no suitable refuge holes are available, they can leap up to 7 feet (2 m) from tree to tree to find a suitable hole. They climb swiftly and keep the tree trunk or branch between them and any possible threat.

Tree squirrels enjoy basking in the sun, especially in the colder winter months, and grooming is very important. This helps to establish and maintain firm bonds between the male and female and their young.

Diet Predominantly vegetarian, tree squirrels eat a wide variety of flowers, seeds, leaves, berries, grasses, fruit, tree resins, and bark. They will also eat ants, termites, aphids, and other insects. Tree squirrels bury hard foods such as seeds and nuts, but they will not bury food in the presence of others in the family group. Although squirrels try to keep the food cache a secret, stealing does occur.

Breeding Parents use a hole in a tree—often an old barbet or woodpecker hole—and line it with grass and leaves to form a nest. The young can be born any time of the year, but generally appear during the wet season.

When born, the infants are blind and sparsely haired. Their eyes open by the eighth day and they develop a wooly coat, which they shed at about two months old. The young emerge from the nest hole at twenty days old, but remain on the trunk and branches where it is safe. At five weeks, the young follow the mother on the ground, foraging and learning what is good to eat. Both parents groom the young.

Kudu and Jackal Go Swimming

(A Swazi story)

One day long ago, Jackal gazed longingly across a broad, swift river at First Man's field of fine maize. He was famished. Food on Jackal's side of the river was scarce. Nearby, Kudu was browsing on some dry, brittle acacia shoots. He, too, was very hungry.

"Friend Kudu," said Jackal, "please carry me across the river so that I may eat at the other side. My legs are too short for me to wade across and I cannot swim for the current is too strong. There are luscious fresh shoots for you to browse on in the bushes, so that both of us will be satisfied."

"Very well," replied Kudu. "I am also hungry."

Kudu knelt down so that Jackal could climb onto his back. Then he carried him across the rushing waters. When Jackal dismounted, he slunk into First Man's maize field and enjoyed an enormous meal.

Kudu meanwhile had his head in the bushes. He was munching on tender green shoots there and enjoying·the good food provided by the Creator.

No sooner had Jackal finished his huge feast than he started howling and dancing with joy.

"What is that dreadful noise?" said First Man. He picked up a large stick and went to investigate. First Man was furious when he saw the damage

done to his crops. Jackal had seen First Man coming. He hid in an aardvark hole so it was Kudu who First Man saw, browsing contentedly nearby. First Man was so angry at the theft of his crops, he beat the innocent Kudu despite his protests.

Then First Man stormed back to his house, leaving a sore and aching Kudu to limp back to the river. Now that it was safe, Jackal ran after Kudu.

"Why did you sing so loudly?" asked Kudu. "Your foolish noise brought the owner and I was beaten for your theft of the maize!"

Jackal laughed, showing no sign of remorse or concern for Kudu's plight. "All my kind dance and sing loudly when our bellies are full of good food. It is our custom!"

"Well, let us return to our side of the river before you cause further trouble," said Kudu, and he knelt down so Jackal could climb onto his back.

Kudu stepped into the swiftly flowing river and the cool water soothed his cuts and bruises. He decided to teach Jackal a lesson for his deceit.

Suddenly, Kudu began to roll from side to side, going down on his knees in preparation to lie down.

"Hey!" cried Jackal. "What are you doing? I will fall into the water and drown if you are not careful!"

Kudu paid no attention to Jackal's complaints. Then Jackal slipped from his back and tumbled into the river. As Jackal struggled to stay afloat, Kudu said calmly, "All my kind roll and bathe in the water when our bellies are filled with good food. It is our custom!"

Kudu's Wonderful Horns

(A Hottentot tale)

Long ago, there was a young boy whose father was a powerful chief. The boy's mother had died giving birth to him and although his father loved him dearly, he was ill-treated by his many relatives.

Because of this bad treatment, the boy decided to leave his father's *kraal*. So he set off on his own to find a new and happier home. The Creator saw and admired the bravery of the young boy and he sent a magnificent kudu bull to protect and provide for him.

The kudu bull found the young boy by a spring, where he was taking a drink. Kudu told the boy he would stay with him and help him in his travels.

The boy and Kudu roamed far and wide across the *veld* in search of a new home. The boy often rode on Kudu's back and whenever he felt hungry he would tap Kudu's right horn and food would magically appear. After satisfying his hunger, he would tap the left horn and the leftover food would disappear.

One day, the boy and Kudu were surprised by a fierce buffalo bull while crossing a thick stand of bush.

"I will fight and overcome this buffalo," Kudu said.

The boy dismounted and a terrible fight took place. At last, the buffalo was defeated and the boy climbed up onto Kudu's back. They continued on their way.

Several days later, the boy and Kudu were surprised by a ferocious lion.

"I shall fight and die here," said Kudu. "You must break off my horns and take them with you. When you are hungry, speak to them and they will supply you with all you need."

In the fight that followed, Kudu was killed as he had predicted. After the lion had gone, the boy recovered Kudu's magnificent horns.

Taking the horns with him, the boy walked on alone. Soon he came to a village. Drought had caused the crops to fail and the people were very hungry.

The chief of the village invited the young boy into his home and offered him a small bowl of soup made of boiled weeds. Seeing how little food they had, the boy spoke to Kudu's horns and called forth enough food for everyone in the village.

One of the villagers saw this miracle and wanted the horns for himself. So that night, he crept into the chief's hut. While the boy slept, he stole the magical horns, replacing them with ordinary kudu horns.

The next morning, the boy set off on his travels. Later that day, as he rested, he called on the horns to provide food, but nothing appeared.

Fearing the worst, the boy retraced his steps to the village. He soon found the thief calling for food from the magical horns, but to no avail. The boy told the chief what had happened and the horns were returned and the thief was punished. In gratitude, the boy called on the horns to provide food for the entire village until the next rains came.

The next day, the boy left the village to continue his search for a new home. At the next village, he asked the headman for shelter. But he was turned away, for now he was dirty and untidy from his long journey.

For many years, the boy traveled, searching for a perfect home. At last, now a young man, he came upon a village whose chief welcomed him into his home. This chief had a beautiful daughter. The young man called on Kudu's horns to provide food, clothing, and ornaments for the girl's family.

A week later, when all the preparations had been made and the dowry was arranged (with the help of Kudu's horns), the young man and the beautiful maiden were married. A huge feast was prepared for the guests, again provided by Kudu's horns.

Shortly after, the young man and his bride returned to his father's village and the old chief received them with honor and joy.

For the last time, the young man spoke to Kudu's horns and called for a home. A spacious *kraal* and new huts magically appeared and fine healthy cattle filled the pens.

It was now that the young man settled down. Close to his father, and with his wife and many children, he found peace and happiness. All thanks to Kudu's wonderful horns.

FACTS ABOUT KUDUS
SPECIES:
GREATER KUDU *(Tragelaphus strepsiceros)*
Males are solitary. Females are gregarious, living in small family herds.

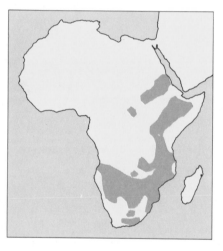

	Male	Female
Height	5 ft	4 ft
Weight	500 lb	400 lb
Weight at Birth	35 lb	35 lb
Age at Weaning	2 months	2 months
Age at Maturity	2 years	18 months
Gestation Period	—	7 months
Number of Young	—	1
Lifespan	8 years	8 years

Identification To many people, the kudu is the most handsome of the antelopes. In males, the body is a fawn gray. Females are tinged with cinnamon and the fawns are even lighter in color. They have six to ten irregular vertical white stripes down their sides.

The neck is long and darker than the body and, in males, it is fringed with dark hair from chin to forequarters. The large ears are a distinctive feature and the face has a white "V" across the forehead. The lips and chin are white.

Males have stately, corkscrew-shaped horns that grow as the animal ages. They can reach a length over the front curve of 5½ feet (1.7 m).

Habitat Kudus are a savanna/woodland species, preferring light forest or thick bush country. They avoid open grassland. Males prefer thicker woodland habitats and most are partial to areas of broken, rocky terrain. Kudus rely on a good source of drinking water.

Habits Greater kudus usually live in small herds or family groups, but males are solitary. From April to June, they form bachelor herds to establish dominance. They then join the small female herds for a short time while mating.

Kudus are most active in the early morning and late afternoon, preferring to rest in the shade during the heat of the day. They are mostly nocturnal where they are subject to heavy hunting by people in and around farming areas.

A shy, retiring species, kudus immediately run for cover if disturbed. The adult males run with their noses straight forward when running through thickets so that their horns lie back along their shoulders to avoid snagging on branches. They have a heavy, rather clumsy gait and their tails curl up when they run, showing the white area underneath.

In woodland, kudus are less nervous and tend to "freeze" to avoid detection. They use their large ears to locate possible danger. Kudus are also accomplished jumpers and can clear a 6½-foot (2 m) high fence with ease.

Diet Kudus browse on shrubs and trees, but they also graze new grass and will raid crops and ornamental plants in some areas.

Breeding A single calf is born during the rainy season when the grass is tallest. The mother leaves the female herd and gives birth in the protective cover of this tall grass. The mother eats the placenta, or afterbirth. This helps to keep predators from being attracted to the site and the calf relies on camouflage and lying motionless to avoid detection.

The calf remains hidden for the first two months. Then the mother introduces the youngster into the herd. By this time, the calf can run quickly and keep up with the other animals.

The calves are a light cinnamon-fawn color, but the white vertical stripes are clear from birth, as is the distinctive V-shaped facial marking.

Why Bushbuck Has a Red Coat

(A story from the Herero)

Long ago, Bushbuck and Impala were good friends and could always be found in each other's company. The other animals often said that they were so alike they must be cousins. In those ancient times, Bushbuck's coat was a sandy color, similar to Impala's.

The rainy season came and Impala had a small baby. She was very proud of her fine, dainty infant. Bushbuck was very kind to Impala and her calf and he was like an uncle to the youngster. Bushbuck would often stand guard over the young impala while it rested, or when his mother went off to feed or get a drink from a nearby pan.

One hot day, the baby impala lay down to sleep in the shade of a big tree. Mother Impala wanted to go and get a drink for she was very thirsty. She asked Bushbuck to watch over her infant as usual. Bushbuck said he would happily stand guard, so Impala trotted off to the waterhole.

Bushbuck browsed lazily on some shrubs nearby. The hot, humid weather made him feel very drowsy and try as he might he could not stay awake. Eventually, he lay down in the shade next to the sleeping youngster and fell asleep.

Nearby, evil old Hyena had been watching Bushbuck. When he was sure that Bushbuck was sound asleep, he quietly ambled up to the sleeping pair.

Seeing such an easy and delicious meal, Hyena snatched up the sleeping young impala and killed him instantly with his powerful jaws. To make sure that he would not be suspected as the culprit, Hyena threw some blood from his victim all over Bushbuck, who had heard nothing and was still fast asleep. Hyena was very pleased with this trick and he ran off with his prey.

When Impala returned from her drink, she was horrified to find no sign of her baby and to see Bushbuck covered in blood from head to foot. Her cry of grief woke Bushbuck with a start. He was aghast to see the state of his coat and that there was no sign of the youngster left in his safekeeping.

Impala assumed the worst, as Hyena had hoped, and drove her friend off with unjust accusations of betrayal.

Today, impalas live in herds of their own kind, for they will only entrust

the safety of their young to other impalas. Also, impala young are active very soon after birth and can follow their mothers wherever they go.

Poor Bushbuck could never prove his innocence. He became a solitary creature, living in thick, overgrown bush away from the impala of the open bush. And since that day, Bushbuck has had a red coat. No matter how hard he tried, he could not clean off the bloodstains and the red color always reminds him of how his negligence failed his trusted friend.

FACTS ABOUT BUSHBUCKS
SPECIES:
BUSHBUCK *(Tragelaphus scriptus)*
Solitary, or in small family groups.

	Male	Female
Height	3 ft	2¼ ft
Weight	110 lb	80 lb
Weight at Birth	8¾ lb	8¾ lb
Age at Weaning	2 months	2 months
Age at Maturity	10 months	14 months
Gestation Period	—	180 days
Number of Young	—	1
Lifespan	9 years	9 years

Identification A medium-size antelope, closely related to the greater kudu. The males have a reddish colored coarse coat and a ridge of white extends along the spine with several indistinct white lines across the lower back. The flanks have conspicuous white spots and the throat has two white bars. The adult female is lighter in color. Their white markings are similar to the males, but the spots on the sides and flanks are less distinct. The young are similar in color to the females.

Only the male bushbuck has horns. These horns are about 1 foot (30 cm) in length, smooth, and roughly triangular at the base. They spiral upwards from the head in rough parallel.

Habitat   The bushbuck is widely distributed throughout the region shown on the map above, but prefers forests or thick bush near a permanent water source.

Habits   Though often seen as solitary animals, bushbucks also live in pairs or small family groups. Sometimes two or more young males will form a small bachelor herd.

Bushbucks generally rest in dense bush during the heat of the day. They feed during the early morning and late afternoon, and at night.

Bushbucks are shy, retiring antelopes with acute senses of smell, hearing, and sight. They grunt to communicate with each other in dense bush.

At any sign of danger, bushbucks utter a loud, hoarse bark as a warning call and will readily take refuge in open water as they are strong swimmers. When cornered or wounded, the males can be very aggressive and dangerous, wielding their sharp horns with great effect.

Diet   Bushbucks are browsers, but on occasion will eat fresh grass. The bulk of the diet consists of leaves, buds, flowers, and fruit from a wide variety of plants. Bushbucks can be a problem in forestry plantations as they stunt the growth of the young trees by nibbling off the tops.

Breeding   The young can be born at any time of the year, though calving is more common in the rainy season. The single youngster is born in dense undergrowth and the female returns to it regularly to suckle it until it is strong enough to move freely with the female.

Duiker Saves Chief Khama I

(A story from the Bamangwato)

This tale, which may have been born in fact, is very dear to the hearts of the Bamangwato Tribe of Botswana. The kindness of the little, shy Duiker so moved Chief Khama I, the Great Grandfather of Khama the Great, that he made Duiker the totem, or emblem, of the Bamangwato Tribe. This is the story of how such a thing came to pass.

During the early 1800s, the ruthless Matabele King, Mzilikazi, was laying waste to vast tracts of land in a terrible war. The Matabele warriors surged through Chief Khama's land like an unstoppable wave, sweeping all before them. The destruction of the Bamangwato army was just one of their many victories.

Chief Khama had been trapped by the encircling Matabele when his warriors fell. He was forced to flee, as a ruler of such an important tribe as the Bamangwato would be a valuable captive.

Chief Khama had to run long and hard, mile after mile, and all the while the relentless Matabele closed in on him. As the chase wore on, Khama's breath became faster and shallower, his strides more labored and he stumbled from exhaustion. A cry of joy from his pursuers stimulated his weary muscles and he ran on.

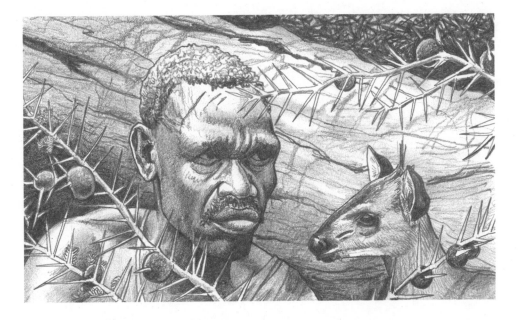

Then Chief Khama saw a large stand of trees and scrub that would hide him from his pursuers. But his chances of reaching this forest haven were small indeed as the Matabele were gaining on him with every step. A tangled clump of thorn bush lay ahead of him and, with a last spurt of energy, Khama threw himself into its dense cover.

Slowly and quietly, Khama wormed his way into the shadows in the center of the thicket. The thorns tore at his flesh, but eventually he eased himself behind a fallen log.

Lying motionless beside the log was another fugitive. Duiker was also nestled there and the little creature did not even flinch when the man brushed past him and hid by his side. The motionless Duiker and the exhausted Chief stared into each other's eyes as the sound of countless Matabele feet thundered toward them like a stampeding herd of buffalo.

The Matabele surrounded the thicket and cried out, "We have him!"

Khama heard them as they started to poke their *assegais* into the thicket. He tried to quiet his thumping heart and hold his ragged breath.

Still, the little Duiker did not move and Khama drew comfort from the warmth of Duiker beside him and the kindness in the soft, dewy eyes of the little antelope.

"He cannot escape us now, for we have him surrounded!" the Matabele warriors shouted. One warrior stabbed his *assegai* into the very log that Chief Khama and Duiker lay behind. The Matabele were sure they had their Chief of the Bamangwato now.

Suddenly Duiker dashed from the thicket. Away through the line of warriors Duiker dodged, as though trying to draw them away.

"Our quarry has escaped us after all!" exclaimed the disappointed warriors. "Duiker does not lie next to a man. Had the one we seek been inside the thicket, Duiker would have fled at his approach. Come, we waste our time—on with the hunt!" And they hastened off towards the forest, not thinking it worthwhile to search the place from which Duiker had bolted.

The Chief of the Bamangwato heaved a sigh of relief. Khama could only feel awe and gratitude for Duiker, who had surely saved his life. Why had such a timid little antelope not made a bid to escape when he, a dreaded human, had pressed so dangerously close to his soft, gray-brown hair? Surely, the Creator had sent Duiker to save him.

FACTS ABOUT DUIKERS
SPECIES:
COMMON OR GRAY DUIKER
(Sylvicapra grimmia)
Solitary, mainly nocturnal.

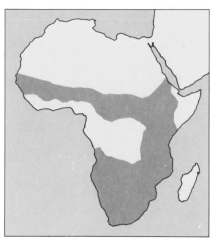

	Male	Female
Height	2 ft	2 ft
Weight	39 lb	44 lb
Weight at Birth	3¼ lb	3¼ lb
Age at Weaning	6 weeks	6 weeks
Age at Maturity	1 year	8–10 months
Gestation Period	—	7 months
Number of Young	—	1
Lifespan	9 years	9 years

Identification The common duiker is a small antelope and has a distinctive black band up its muzzle, from the base of the black nose to the forehead. There is a long tuft of dark hair on the forehead and a dark band on the front of the forelegs. Color varies from a grayish-buff to a reddish-yellow. The underneath is a uniform whitish color. There is little color variation between males, females, and young.

Only the male duikers have the short straight horns that are heavily ridged. The record size is 7½ inches (18 cm).

Habitat Common duikers inhabit bush country, as they require cover to forage in. They are not generally found on open grasslands. They can occur from sea level up to 6000 feet (1800 m).

Habits Normally solitary, although pairs can be seen during the mating season or mothers can be seen with their young. They are mainly active during the night, but will forage in the early morning and late afternoon. They rest during the heat of the day in thick bush and tall grass.

The duiker is usually a quiet animal, but can give a nasal snort as an alarm call. When disturbed, duikers "freeze" and if they feel threatened, they make off at high speed in a series of plunging jumps. Then they dive for the nearest dense cover, hence their name, from the Afrikaans "duik" or "to dive."

The duiker can survive in agricultural lands and even on the fringes of urban areas.

Diet Duikers are essentially browsers and rarely eat grasses. Their diet consists of leaves, buds, flowers, twigs, seeds, and fruit. They will also dig for tubers and roots and nibble at the bark of trees. They have been known to damage saplings in forestry areas as well as commercial crops.

Breeding The duiker can have young at any time of the year and a single offspring is born in the cover of dense vegetation. After cleaning, the mother leaves the newborn animal hidden, returning from time to time to suckle it. The young duiker is very active after the first day and if it is not happy with its den, it will move to a new site nearby, which the female soon finds. Shortly after birth, the youngster accompanies the female in her foraging and it starts to take solid food after the first month.

When Lion Could Fly
(and Why Vulture Scavenges)

(An ancient Hottentot tale)

In the beginning, Lion possessed great magic, which gave him the power of flight. All the beasts of the earth and the sky lived in dread of Lion.

Lion was such a ferocious hunter that no animal was safe from his huge appetite. Beside his lair, he had built a great graveyard with all the bones from his kills.

Lion was very proud of his prowess as a hunter and he enslaved a pair of Vultures to guard over this monument to his power. Secretly, however, Lion feared that the bones in his graveyard would be broken and scattered as this was where he hid his bundle of magical treasures that gave him the gift of flight.

One morning, when Lion had flown off on his daily hunting expedition, the Vultures, who were unable to fly in those days, were guarding the vast pile of bones. As the morning wore on, the Vultures grew bored. Suddenly, Bullfrog leapt into Lion's lair and, despite the alarmed Vultures' protests, the huge frog started to scatter and break the collection of bones.

"Why should all live in fear of one!" croaked Bullfrog. "If your master is so

great, let him come and devour me. I will wait for him at his drinking pool." And off he hopped.

The Vultures were beside themselves with fear. What would Lion do to them when he saw what was left of his bone display? As they looked dismally over the wreckage, they spotted Lion's magic bundle. The Vultures opened it and ate up all the contents. To their immense relief, they now had the power of flight. To escape from Lion's wrath, they soared up into the heavens.

Meanwhile, Lion had been lying in ambush waiting for his next meal. When some buffalo ventured nearby, Lion tried to soar into the sky and swoop down on the unsuspecting beasts in his usual manner. But without his magical power, Lion was unable to take off. He became very, very angry and ran back to his lair to see what was wrong.

Lion was overcome with rage when he saw the wreckage. Looking up, he spied the Vultures circling high above. Lion roared at them to explain the devastation. The Vultures told Lion of Bullfrog's actions and the message he had left.

"Come here, you stupid fowl," ordered Lion, who wanted to teach the Vultures a lesson. The Vultures, however, were not so foolish as to obey, and rising higher on a column of warm air they circled off over the *veld*.

Remembering Bullfrog's message, Lion ran down to the nearby pool. He was going to make someone pay for his lost magic. Seeing Bullfrog sitting on the edge of the pool, Lion crept up to his intended prey. Bullfrog saw Lion's reflection in the mirror-like pool and leapt out of harm's way.

Try as he might, Lion could not get close enough to catch Bullfrog, who leapt away effortlessly every time Lion approached. Eventually, Lion became exhausted. Worn out beyond anger, he gave up his chase.

Slowly Lion began to plod back to his ruined lair. Then Bullfrog called out, "Ho, King of the Beasts! Now that your magic has gone you must hunt like all other earthbound animals."

So it has been ever since. Lion can only roam the Earth in search of prey, whereas Vulture can now soar in the skies. But Vulture still fears Lion, and only comes to Earth to scavenge carrion when Lion has had his fill.

Why There Are Cracks in Tortoise's Shell

(A story from the Barotse)

In the beginning, Tortoise's best friend was Vulture. Vulture was always visiting Tortoise, but as Tortoise was very slow he was unable to go and visit Vulture. This upset Tortoise a great deal.

One day, Tortoise said to his wife, "I am worried that we will lose the friendship of Vulture if we do not visit him at his house and repay his courtesy. He is always coming here and yet I have never been to visit him and he is my best friend."

"I don't see how Vulture could think badly of us as he knows we are not gifted with the power of flight," replied Tortoise's wife.

"Nevertheless, I feel terrible about my shortcoming!" Tortoise said sadly.

Tortoise pondered over his dilemma for a long time. Then he had an idea.

"As I cannot fly, Wife, wrap me in a bundle of your woven reed mats. When Vulture arrives, give it to him as a gift from us for his house."

And this is exactly what Tortoise's wife did. Then she placed the bundle of mats in the corner of her yard. When Vulture arrived to pay his daily visit, he looked around for his friend. Not seeing him he asked, "Where has your husband gone?"

Tortoise's wife said Tortoise had had to run an errand for her and sent his apologies for missing his friend. As a token of their friendship, she said that Tortoise wanted Vulture to take the bundle of woven reed mats for his home.

Thanking her, Vulture happily took the parcel and flew off to his house. As he flew, Vulture gripped the bundle in his sharp, powerful talons. When Vulture neared his house, Tortoise called out from the bundle, "Untie me, I am your friend Tortoise. Did I not promise you that one day I would visit your home!"

Unfortunately Vulture received such a shock at hearing the voice coming from the bundle in his talons, that he let go of the bundle and Tortoise fell to the earth. His hard, smooth shell was smashed to bits and he did not survive the fall.

From that day on, like the shell, the friendship between Tortoise and Vulture was broken. And today, you can still see the cracks in the shells of Tortoise's descendants.

FACTS ABOUT VULTURES
SPECIES:
WHITEBACKED VULTURE *(Gyps africanus)*

Gregarious, less so during breeding season.

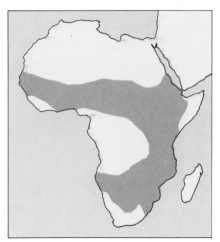

	Male	Female
Length	3 ft	3¼ ft
Wing span	7 ft	7¼ ft
Weight	11 lb	13 lb
Weight at Hatching	5 oz	5 oz
Age at Maturity	8 years	8 years
Incubation period	—	57 days
	(incubated by both sexes)	
Number of Eggs	—	1
Lifespan	30 years	30 years

Identification This large vulture is the most common in southern Africa. The body plumage is brown and is faintly streaked.   The eyes are dark, the face is blackish, and the bare neck is pink. The lower back has a conspicuous white patch that can be seen when the adult bird flies. The young are darker than their parents.

Habitat The whitebacked vulture is found on savannas and bush country. Persecution by people means most vultures are now confined to national parks and areas of remote wilderness.

Habits These gregarious birds roost in large groups in trees at night and soar out soon after sunrise to forage. Vultures can glide at about 38 miles per hour (60 kph) and can dive at up to 75 miles an hour (120 kph).

They have sharp eyesight and watch out for other vultures, crows, kites, and even hyenas and lions, to locate food on the plains.

When they gather at a carcass, they are very aggressive and noisy. New arrivals bound in with wings and neck outstretched and many noisy squabbles occur as the fittest compete for the best food.

Vultures often rest on the ground during the day and drink and bathe in pans regularly.

Diet Vultures are exclusively scavengers and have a diet of carrion and bone fragments—mainly from the softer parts of game animals. Bone fragments, usually provided after hyenas have crunched up bones with their powerful jaws, are essential, especially for developing chicks, to promote healthy bone growth.

Breeding A nesting platform is made of sticks and lined with grass and green leaves. The nest is usually 16 to 40 inches across (40 to 100 cm) and often on top of large acacia trees 26 to 160 feet (8 to 50 m) above the ground. The nest is usually in a small, loosely associated nesting colony, but can occur alone.

A single white egg is laid in the winter and both parents will incubate the egg. Incubation takes 56 to 58 days and the chick starts calling two days before hatching. It can take three days to complete the difficult hatching process.

Both parents feed the chick, which grows rapidly. Within 45 days it can feed itself from the chewed up food brought back to the nest by the parents. The youngster leaves the nest about four months after its first flight.

Why Guinea Fowl Calls at Dawn (and Why Flies Buzz)

(An Ekoi tale)

The Ekoi of Nigeria tell us that Guinea Fowl is always the first creature to wake among all the creatures of the bush. Her raucous calls raise the sun from its nightly rest. Guinea Fowl then rises into the sky and a new day begins.

One day, First Man and First Woman went into the forest to collect food. They found a grove of palm trees with clusters of ripe dates. First Man climbed to the top of the nearest palm tree and began hacking with his knife at the heavy clusters of dates.

This disturbed a swarm of small black flies, which then buzzed annoyingly around First Man's face and tickled his nose. First Man tried to brush them off, but he slipped and dropped his knife.

First Man yelled a warning to his wife below and she leapt quickly out of harm's way. But in doing so, she jumped over Cobra who was sleeping beneath some fallen leaves. Cobra was so frightened that he dived into a nearby hole.

This hole was Rat's home. Poor Rat received such a scare from his unwelcome visitor that he dashed out of his hole and sought safety in the nearest tree.

Unfortunately Rat chose the tree that Weaver Bird nested in. Fearing that Rat was trying to steal his eggs, he set up a dreadful racket.

This screaming and cackling terrified the wits out of Colobus Monkey who was sitting in a neighboring tree. In shock, he dropped the juicy mango he was about to eat for lunch.

The mango fell and landed with a thud on Elephant's head, who was peacefully dozing in the tree's shade. Thinking that hunters were after him, Elephant stampeded off. But Elephant had hooked a sturdy liana with his tusks. In his flight, he uprooted the tree and dragged it off through the bush.

The roots of the liana were embedded in a tall ant heap. Elephant's charge pulled the roots free and the ant heap fell onto Guinea Fowl's nest, breaking all her eggs.

Poor Guinea Fowl was so upset by the loss of her clutch of eggs that she spread her feathers out over the ruined nest and did not utter a sound for two whole days and nights. Sun was not woken each morning by her calls and so all the land was in darkness. The other animals feared this darkness and cried out to the Creator to save them.

The Creator summoned all the animals together. "Why have you not wakened the sun these past two mornings?" the Creator asked Guinea Fowl.

"My eggs were broken by a falling ant heap, that was pulled over by a creeper, that was dragged away by Elephant, who was hit by a mango, that was dropped by Colobus Monkey, who was startled by Weaver Bird, who was frightened by Rat, who was scared by Cobra, who was woken by First Woman, who was avoiding a knife that was dropped by her husband, who was annoyed by some small black flies, who live at the top of a palm tree," wailed Guinea Fowl.

The Creator went back through the unfortunate chain of events, questioning each animal and confirming all the details. Eventually the Creator came to the culprits, the small black flies.

"It seems to me that you are the cause of all the trouble," said the Creator to the small black flies. "Why did you annoy First Man as he went about his food gathering?" he demanded. Instead of answering courteously, as all the other animals had done, the black flies only flew around saying, "Buzz,

buzz, buzz!" The Creator repeated his question and ordered the small black flies to speak. But he was answered again by an annoying BUZZ!

"Because you refuse to answer my question, I now take away your powers of speech. From now onwards you shall only be capable of buzzing!"

Turning to Guinea Fowl, the Creator said, "Never again must you neglect to call the sun at dawn, whatever may have happened to your eggs!"

So it has been ever since. The small black flies never got their voices back and can do nothing but buzz. And Guinea Fowl has always called out to start a new day.

FACTS ABOUT GUINEA FOWLS
SPECIES:
HELMETED GUINEA FOWL
(Numida meleagris)
Highly gregarious, especially out of the breeding season.

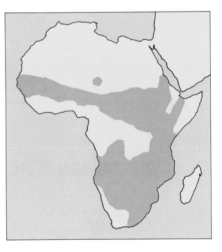

	Male	Female
Length	2 ft	1¼ ft
Wing span	11 in	10 in
Weight	4 lb	2¾ lb
Weight at hatching	⅔ oz	⅔ oz
Age at Maturity	1 year	1 year
Incubation Period	—	26 days
Number of Eggs	—	6–19
Lifespan	5 years	5 years

Identification Similar in size to a domestic hen. The plumage is slate gray with many fine white spots. The head and neck are bare and the skin is blue and red. The adults have a conspicuous horny helmet-like structure called a casque on top of their heads, which grows with age. The young are browner in color, with a downy neck and a smaller casque.

Habitat Open grasslands, *vleis*, savannas, cultivated lands, edges of scrub and bush. The guinea fowl has adapted to living in and around farmlands and has increased its range as people have moved into new areas.

Habits Guinea fowl are highly gregarious birds when they are not breeding. They gather in flocks, which may number several hundred birds. These flocks forage on open ground, scratching for food with their feet or bills. The males often chase each other, especially before the breeding season. Guinea fowl can run fast when disturbed and can also fly well.

They usually roost communally at night in trees.

Guinea fowl are very dependent on water and usually walk in single file to water-holes, forming long processions.

The guinea fowl is a noisy bird and will utter raucous, rattling "kek kek" alarm calls.

Diet Guinea fowl eat a wide range of bulbs, tubers, seeds, berries, snails, insects, ticks, and millipedes. As they eat a lot of harmful pests, the birds are welcomed by farmers.

Breeding Pairs separate from the flock during the rainy season. The peak breeding time usually occurs during the peak rains (mainly during November to January in southern Africa).

A shallow nest is scraped in the ground and lined with dry grass. It is usually in dense cover under grass and scrub. The creamy-white eggs have large brownish pore marks and are sometimes finely speckled.

The female incubates the eggs, but the male will help to care for the chicks. The young can fly at fourteen days, but only weakly. They are fully fledged at four weeks old.

Honeyguide's Revenge

(A tale from the Ndebele)

One day, in the most ancient of times, Honeyguide found a lovely old beehive that was dripping with honey. As Honeyguide could not reach the honey alone, he searched the bush for someone that he could lead to the spot to help rob the hive. Then Honeyguide would have his favorite meal—honey and bee grubs.

Eventually Honeyguide found First Man. He guided him through the bush, often stopping to sing his honey song.

> *"Quiri ra makuti, makuti, makuti—den den den,*
> *Tsa-tsaga-tsa, gwarang-ga, quiri ra."*

Soon Honeyguide had led First Man to the beehive. First Man quickly made a smoky fire to make the bees drowsy. Though First Man got stung a few times, he did not mind. A hive full of sweet, sticky honey was worth a bit of discomfort!

First Man was so overjoyed with the thought of providing such a treat for his family that his heart filled with greed. He scraped the hive clean and placed the wax combs and honey into a huge gourd, or calabash, to carry home. He even gathered up the honey drops that fell as he worked and he did not spare a thought for his feathered guide.

When First Man had finished, he went to give his family the good news about the honey. Honeyguide hopped about the ground around the hive, hoping to find at least one morsel. But he found not a single drop of honey or even a solitary grub for all his efforts. Honeyguide was filled with rage and he vowed that he would punish First Man for his selfish greed.

Honeyguide searched the bush for many days and in time he saw exactly what he wanted. Honeyguide had found a mother Leopard with her two newborn cubs concealed beneath a fallen tree trunk. Now Honeyguide's plot was ready and he gleefully flew off to First Man's home.

Flying and diving low past First Man's ear, Honeyguide gave a "che-che-che" call to attract his foe's attention. Making sure that he slipped away unnoticed, First Man gladly followed Honeyguide.

As Honeyguide sang his honey song again, First Man plotted to keep the spoils to himself. This time he would not even share it with his family—such

was his lust for one of nature's greatest gifts. For mile after mile he followed Honeyguide, until the bird perched right above Leopard's lair.

"Ah ha!" said First Man. "My walk ends here!" He stepped onto the fallen trunk, thinking that it would make his climb up the tree to the beehive easier. Leopard and her cubs blended in so perfectly with the shadows that First Man nearly stood on one of the tiny cubs. With a savage snarl, Leopard sprang.

Who can fight Leopard without any weapons, especially when she is defending her young? First Man's end was as swift as it was terrible. And so Honeyguide had his revenge.

To this day, First Man's descendants respect Honeyguide. Whenever he guides them to a beehive, they always leave behind a piece or two of Honeyguide's favorite food—honey and bee grubs. They fear that if Honeyguide does not get his just reward, the cunning little bird could lead them into a terrible trap as he did First Man.

The Birds' Great Race

(A story from the Bushman)

Long ago, when all the birds were equal upon the Earth, the feathered creatures were always quarreling among themselves. The Creator decided that the birds should have a Chief—a bird with wisdom and cunning to settle arguments and keep the peace.

The Creator called together all the birds and told them of his plan. To select the Chief, there would be a great race the following day. As the sun reached its highest point in the sky, they were all to fly up into the heavens. The first bird to touch the Creator's outstretched hand would become Chief of all the feathered creatures.

There was great excitement among the birds. Everyone expected Martial Eagle to win, thanks to his strong muscles and great powerful wings. There was a cruel glint in Martial Eagle's yellow eyes as he thought of having power over all the other birds. All those who saw this terrible look trembled.

But not so Honeyguide. He often went unnoticed. He was too small to be seen among the likes of Crowned Crane, Gray Heron, Flamingo, Ground Hornbill, Kori Bustard, Crimson-Breasted Shrike, and Oriole, all of whom were either big or bright and colorful.

Honeyguide knew he was quick enough to avoid the cruel strike of Martial Eagle's wicked talons—and he had a scheme. With bright little eyes, the wise Honeyguide hopped around as cocky as ever.

The next day at noon, all the birds were assembled at the appointed place. All, that is, except for Ostrich, who was a bit dim-witted. Ostrich had forgotten all about the contest. This made the Creator so cross at Ostrich's forgetfulness that he took away Ostrich's power of flight forever.

As the sun reached its highest point, the Creator sent a great clap of thunder and the vast flock of birds rose into the sky. No one gave a thought to Honeyguide, least of all Martial Eagle, but the tiny bird was there.

As Martial Eagle spread his wings to rise, Honeyguide shot like an arrow onto Martial Eagle's shoulder and clung on for dear life. Martial Eagle shook himself, thinking to dislodge a troublesome fly. But the "fly" clung on and Martial Eagle, ignoring this slight irritation, settled down for a long flight.

Higher and higher rose the great column of birds. The veld was soon out of sight as they rose ever upward. After a while, the birds began to fly slower and slower as their wings grew tired.

But not so Martial Eagle. His powerful wings drove him upward. One by one, the exhausted birds tired. Some fell way behind, some gave up entirely, and others struggled gamely on. Martial Eagle led them all. Finally, he was the only one left in the Great Race. Or, at least he *thought* he was the only one left in the Great Race.

With only a few yards to go to the waiting outstretched hand of the Creator, Martial Eagle slackened his speed. This was his undoing, as Honey guide took off like a streak of lightning from Martial Eagle's shoulder and flew straight into the Creator's open hand. Honeyguide had won the race.

"Such brains and daring deserve to lead the feathered ones!" said the Creator. "Do not always look to size and strength for wisdom and cunning!"

FACTS ABOUT HONEYGUIDES
SPECIES:
GREATER HONEYGUIDE
(Indicator indicator)
Usually solitary.

	Male	Female
Length	8 in	7½ in
Wing span	4½ in	4¼ in
Weight	2 oz	1¾ oz
Weight at hatching	⅕ oz	⅕ oz
Age at Maturity	1 year	1 year
Number of Eggs	—	1 egg per host nest (up to 8 in all)
Lifespan	5 years	5 years

Identification This is the largest of the honeyguides of southern Africa. They are drab, inconspicuous birds; dark gray above and light gray below. The male has a large white ear patch and black throat that the female lacks. Both have a white wing pattern which is conspicuous in flight. The young are browner than the adults and are yellowish in color from chin to breast.

Habitat Widespread but not numerous, greater honeyguides are found in most areas south of the Sahara. These habitats include woodlands, savannas, plantations, farm yards, and orchards, but not semi-deserts.

Habits These birds are usually solitary. The male has a fixed calling site, often high up in a tall tree. Honeyguides are normally silent and unseen except when singing for a mate or when guiding people and honey badgers to beehives. People have taken advantage of this trait of guiding for thousands of years. There is no satisfactory evidence to suggest that honeyguide will lead people deliberately into danger.

Diet Insects, including adult and larval bees, and beeswax.

Breeding Like cuckoos, honeyguides do not rear their own young or incubate their own eggs. After mating with the male at his singing post, the female will lay a single white egg in the nest of other hole-nesting species, such as kingfishers, bee-eaters, hoopoes, swallows, martins, and some starlings and sparrows. While she lays her egg, the female often destroys the eggs of the host bird.

When the nestling hatches it has a hooked bill, which it may use to kill the host bird's young. The incubation and fledging times of the greater honeyguide are not known.

The Hare and the Crocodile

(A Hambakushu legend)

Most tribespeople of Africa fear crocodiles, not only because they are dangerous, but because they believe that crocodiles have evil magical powers. The Shona tribe believe that the skin, bones, and skull of the crocodile must be returned to the water after it has been killed to make certain that rains will fall.

Long, long ago, Ngando the Crocodile lived in a quiet backwater in the swamps of the Great Okavango. One day, a herd of Zebra came down to drink at his creek. Ngando was envious of their grace and beauty and of the freedom with which they roamed the plains. He was bored with his little stretch of water, so he asked the Zebras if he could live with them on the open grasslands.

"How could you live with us?" asked the Zebras. "The plains are so far away from water."

"Oh, I'm sure I will be able to manage," replied Ngando, more hopefully than truthfully.

So when the Zebras filed away after their drink, Ngando the Crocodile heaved himself up the bank and followed them. Soon, he was left far behind and the Zebras had to wait for him to catch up.

By noon, it was so hot that Ngando could go no further. He dug himself in beneath a shady tree. He was so tired he slept as though he was dead. When one of the Zebras returned to look for him, he thought the crocodile had indeed died. So the Zebra left him where he was.

While Ngando slept, Hare strolled past. Hare saw the adventurous crocodile sleeping beneath the shady tree. Hare woke him up (very carefully!), and asked him why he was so far from his home in the water.

"I foolishly followed the Zebras. But they ran off and left me all alone," said Ngando. "I would be very grateful for some assistance in getting home," he added, hopefully.

Hare offered to help, provided Ngando promised him a favor in return. The desperate crocodile quickly agreed and Hare ran off to get help.

Hare cautiously approached his mortal enemy, Hyena. He told him that there was a dead crocodile nearby and that he needed help to carry the body back to the water so as not to anger the Rain Spirits.

Hyena thought this would be an excellent chance to get an easy meal. That was why he agreed to help Hare instead of eating him up.

Hare and Hyena—a most unlikely pair—struggled to carry the heavy crocodile back to the water. At last they arrived and lowered him into the shallows.

Hyena suggested that they leave Ngando in the water for a while so that when they came back he would be nice and tender to eat.

Hyena marked the bank so he would know where to return. Then he slunk away to rest. He wanted to be ready for the huge feast that night.

But Ngando had different plans. As soon as he had cooled down and recovered from his foolhardy adventure, he swam back to his lair.

When Hyena returned after his nap, the "dead" crocodile was nowhere to be seen. Hyena, whose mouth was watering at the thought of a tasty meal, waded into the water to see if his dinner had floated out into the creek. He was searching the water so intently, that he did not notice Ngando silently gliding up behind him. Only Ngando's eyes and the tips of his nostrils were showing.

With a lunge as quick as lightning, Ngando grabbed Hyena with his huge jaws and dragged him into the deep water, where he drowned.

Ngando climbed out onto the river bank to thank Hare for helping him back to the pool where he belonged. Hare replied that Ngando had already returned the favor by ridding him of his worst enemy, Hyena.

Since that time, Crocodile and his descendants have been content to live in the water. You may find them lurking there in the shallows, waiting patiently to pounce upon their unsuspecting prey.

FACTS ABOUT CROCODILES
SPECIES:
NILE CROCODILE *(Crocodylus niloticus)*

Gregarious, but territorial while breeding.

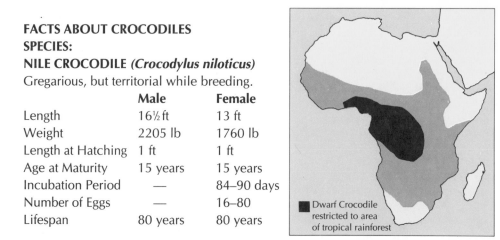

Dwarf Crocodile
restricted to area
of tropical rainforest

	Male	Female
Length	16½ ft	13 ft
Weight	2205 lb	1760 lb
Length at Hatching	1 ft	1 ft
Age at Maturity	15 years	15 years
Incubation Period	—	84–90 days
Number of Eggs	—	16–80
Lifespan	80 years	80 years

Identification   A true "living fossil," geological evidence shows that the crocodile has changed little in the last 65 million years.

The jaws are long and have prominent teeth. The fourth tooth on the lower jaw is visible when the jaw is closed (unlike the North American alligator). The eyes and nostrils are on top of the head.

The skin is covered with horny plates, many of which are ridged and bony. The hind feet are webbed and the huge muscular tail makes up nearly half of the total body length.

Adults are a dark, uniform olive green to gray color, whereas the belly is yellow or creamy colored. The young are greener with black markings.

Habitat   Larger rivers, lakes, dams, and swamps, but also river mouths, and mangrove swamps. The crocodile has been exterminated in many areas as it has been killed for its skin, which is considered fashionable.

Habits   Young crocodiles dig a burrow, sometimes communally, up to 10 feet (3 m) long and use this burrow for the first four to five years. They spend a lot of time out of the water.

Young adults live in the swamps and backwaters, whereas older crocodiles live in more open waterfront and river areas.

On hot days, the older adult crocodiles come ashore to bask, often in large numbers. When the temperature rises, they lie motionless with their mouths ajar, to lose excess heat by evaporation.

They swim effortlessly using their broad, flattened tail. The webbed hind feet are used for careful maneuvering. The crocodile has valves on its nostrils and throat that close, allowing the animal to submerge and even feed underwater:

Diet Baby crocodiles eat insects, fish, and tadpoles. Young adults eat fish, birds, and small mammals. Fully-grown adults eat fish and also ambush game when they drink. Even zebra and buffalo can be taken by large individuals. Attacks on people are still fairly common.

Crocodiles swallow stones to help grind up their food, making it easier to digest. These stones also serve as ballast.

Breeding Following an elaborate courtship and mating, which takes place in the water, the female selects a suitable sunny sand bank above floodwater level. With her back legs, she digs a hole about 16 inches (40 cm) deep, usually at night, and lays her 16 to 80 white, hard-shelled eggs.

Though the male remains in the vicinity, the female will not allow him near the nest mound. When the eggs are ready to hatch, about 90 days later, the hatchlings give a high-pitched cheeping noise that can be heard 65 feet (20 m) away.

The female, who has guarded the nest mound all this time, carefully opens up the nest and, picking up the young with extreme care, takes them down to the water in her mouth. The young stay in a safe area protected by the mother for six to eight weeks. During this stage they are easy prey, especially to *leguaans* and marabou storks.

The sex of the young crocodiles is determined by temperature during incubation. Females are produced at lower temperatures, approximately 79 to 86°F (26 to 30°C), and males at higher temperatures, approximately 88 to 93°F (31 to 34°C).

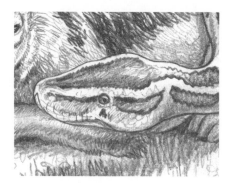

Python Saves the Animals

(A Swazi story)

Before humans were upon the Earth, there was peace, harmony, and friendliness among all the animals. The oldest and wisest animal was an enormous Python. He was very, very old. He was old even before the other animals were created. They believed that Python had been upon the Earth from the beginning of time.

Python knew the names of all the trees, plants, grasses, and their fruits. He also knew which fruits were poisonous and he warned the other animals not to eat any fruit without first asking him if it was safe to eat.

Python lived coiled around a tall qunube tree. The tree was actually a berry bush, but because Python's great body had always supported its many stems, it had grown upward. Python had grown with the qunube tree. There was no need to leave it, for he fed all year on its juicy black berries.

One year, a terrible drought brought starvation to the Earth. The only tree that was still green and full of fruit was Python's qunube tree. Everyone knew that it was Python's tree and because he was so big and powerful, no one dared to ask him if they could share the juicy berries.

As the drought wore on, however, the animals became desperate. They were all starving and dying from thirst. They held a meeting and decided to send a messenger to Python to ask the name of the tree and, more importantly, whether Python would be so kind as to share the fruit with them.

First they sent Cane Rat. Python received him kindly and told him the

name of the tree. "Yes, the other creatures can certainly share the fruit," Python said.

Cane Rat raced back to the other creatures full of excitement. But he was thinking of his empty stomach and when he arrived back he had forgotten the message. The other animals were angry and drove Cane Rat away.

Next they sent Impala. Python was amazed at Cane Rat's stupidity, but he gave the same message to Impala. On his way back, Impala discovered a few morsels of his favorite food. He rushed over to eat it. By the time he started his journey again, Impala, too, had forgotten Python's message.

Poor Impala was driven out by the angry animals.

Finally, they pleaded with their King, Lion, to undertake this mission. (In those early days Lion ate only grass or fruit, like all his subjects.)

Python was amazed and angry that he had to be disturbed once again, but out of kindness he told Lion the tree's name and gave his permission for all to come and share the fruit. As Lion was returning, he was so weak from hunger that he fell down and went to sleep. When he awoke, Lion also had forgotten the message. Lion crept back to the meeting place, ashamed and disgraced.

Even their trusted King had failed them. The animals were dismayed, angry, and full of despair. Finally, Tortoise stepped forward and said he would ask Python. The animals had no faith in Tortoise and only let him go because of his insistence.

This time Python completely lost his patience and said, "How stupid you all are! You deserve to starve for such foolishness. I gave you three chances. I will not tell you the name of my qunube tree again!"

Tortoise has a small head, but a sharp brain. He went back to the other animals as fast as he could go (which was not very fast at all!), and as he went he made up a song to make sure that he would not forget.

> Qunube, Qunube, Qunube,
> O King, what shall we eat?
> Qunube, Qunube, Qunube,
> All the "clever" ones forget,
> Qunube, Qunube, Qunube,
> The tree that will save us all!

When Tortoise returned and sang his song to the animals they all stampeded over to Python's tree. Python was still angry with them. "You all have such short memories, except for Tortoise. He shall have his fill first!"

Python hoisted Tortoise high up into the branches so he could eat his fill of the juicy black berries. When Tortoise was satisfied and full, Python uncoiled his great body and left all the animals to eat to their hearts' content. Python never returned to his qunube tree.

The long awaited rains came soon after, filling the streams and rivers. Python went to live in a deep pool where today his descendants can be found, basking in the dappled sunlight. The qunube tree, no longer supported by Python's great body, dropped down to the ground and formed the berry bushes that are so important as a source of food to many wild creatures today.

Why Python Can Shed His Skin

(A tale from the Mende)

According to the Mende of Sierra Leone in West Africa, there was no Death in the beginning. Death lived with the Creator who was unwilling to let Death go about in the world. Death pleaded with the Creator to be allowed to go down to Earth and eventually the Creator agreed.

At the same time the Creator made a promise to First Man. Although Death had been given permission to roam the Earth, people would not die. The Creator also vowed to send some new skins, which First Man and his family could put on when their bodies grew old. They would then be rejuvenated and therefore cheat Death.

The Creator put the skins into a basket and asked Jackal to take it to First Man and his family. During the journey, Jackal became very hungry. Fortunately, Jackal met some other animals who were having a big feast and they invited him to join them. When Jackal had eaten his fill, he went into the shade and lay down to rest.

While Jackal was dozing, cunning Python approached him and asked what he had in the basket. Jackal told Python what was in the basket and

why he was taking it to First Man. When Jackal feel asleep, Python picked up the basket and slid silently into the jungle.

When Jackal awoke, he discovered that Python had stolen the basket of skins. He ran to First Man and told him what had happened. First Man went to the Creator and told him what had befallen his gift of new skins. He demanded that Python return the basket and its contents. But the Creator said that he would not take back his skins from Python as First Man always demanded more of the Creator than any other animal. So people would have to die when they became old.

From that day on, people bore a grudge against jackals and all snakes. They always tried to kill them whenever they saw them.

This greatly displeased the Creator. So he gave Jackal the gift of cunning in order to survive the wrath of humans. Python, for his part, always avoids people and lives alone. Because Python still has the basket of skins provided by the Creator, he can always shed his old skin for a new one.

FACTS ABOUT PYTHONS
SPECIES:
AFRICAN ROCK PYTHON (Python sebae)
Solitary, non-venomous.

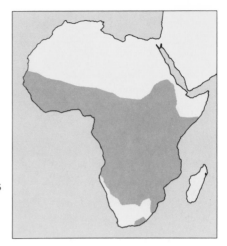

	Male	Female
Length	20 ft	20 ft
Weight	120 lb	120 lb
Length at Hatching	2 ft	2 ft
Age at Maturity	—	65–80 days
Number of Eggs	—	30–50
Lifespan	20 years	20 years

Identification The African rock python is Africa's largest snake and it is very solid and stoutly built. The python has a large triangular head, small scales, and a body that is gray-green or gray-brown with dark brown, black-edged bars and blotches. The belly is white with dark speckles. The young are usually brighter in color.

Pythons have heat sensitive pits on or between the lip scales that detect heat. This allows them to "see" warm-blooded prey in the dark or even when blind.

Habitat Pythons are found in warmer areas, preferring open savannas, rock areas, and bush near rivers. They are particularly fond of water. Pythons are absent only from very arid areas and dense rainforest.

Habits The African rock python is a protected species. Although it is a valuable aid to farmers because it eats many pests, most large pythons have been exterminated. In the past, its skin was much sought after for handbags, belts, and shoes.

Pythons often bask in the sun, especially after feeding or when sloughing (shedding their skins).

They often hunt from the water. They ambush their prey and crush it before swallowing it whole. Pythons, like most snakes, can dislocate their jaws to allow them to swallow prey much larger than their heads.

Python have large teeth and can inflict painful bites when they have to defend themselves.

Diet Adults eat small bucks, monkeys, rodents, dassies, fish, *leguaans* and even crocodiles. The python is the only snake large enough to consider humans as prey, but attacks on people are exceptionally rare, especially as so few large pythons are left.

Breeding The female lays between 30 and 50 large eggs in caves, termite mounds, or abandoned aardvark burrows. A very large female may lay up to 100 eggs, which can weigh 5 ounces (150 g) each and are the size of an orange.

The female coils around her clutch to protect them, but does not incubate them as a bird does. The young hatch after about three and a half months. After hatching, the young fend for themselves.

Chameleon and First Man

(A story from the Ndebele)

In the beginning, when the Creator was completing his plans for the world, he wished to give the gift of immortality to First Man.

The Creator sent Chameleon to First Man with the message that First Man must drink from a stream that he had blessed with heavenly knowledge. After doing so, humankind would live forever.

It was many, many days before Chameleon, or "Slow Walker" as he is also known, completed his task. Chameleon would place one foot in front of the other, then pull it back to ponder on whether he should go forward or backward. Chameleon would do this two, three, or even four times before eventually taking a step forward.

Traveling in such a manner, it took Chameleon a very, very long time to reach the house of First Man. When he told him of the Creator's gift, First Man rushed down to the stream. But he saw no sign of water, only a dry river bed.

First Man found a damp patch of sand and pressed his lips to it, but no water came. Next he pressed the palms of his hands and the soles of his feet to the damp sand, but no water would come. First Man even sucked on damp pebbles, but there was no way he could get enough moisture. He had lost the gift of immortality.

First Man was angry with Chameleon. His slowness meant the loss of ever-lasting life. In his rage, he killed Chameleon.

To this day, many people still kill chameleons on sight, remembering their loss. But the Creator took pity on Chameleon and gave him the gift of a skin that could change color, as if by magic. This now helps the "Slow Walker" to hide from the people's wrath.

Chameleon and the Greedy Spider

(A Bushman legend)

Long ago, in the most ancient of times, the great, great grandfather of all spiders lived in a huge web in a massive tree on the edge of the vast Okavango Swamps. This fat spider was completely round and, as he was always hungry, there was nothing he loved more than a feast.

Spider boasted that he knew everything that was going on in the bush and he made it his business to hide in unexpected places and eavesdrop on what everybody had to say. Most particularly, he spied on the Bees, who traveled far and wide and brought news from the furthermost places. Ants were also very wise and knew all sorts of secrets.

"They say there is to be a feast at …" Ant began to whisper.

"What'll I do? What'll I do?" cooed the Green Pigeon, "What'll I do?"

"Oh, bother that stupid bird," spluttered Spider. "I did not hear where the feast will be!"

Spider was furious. He knew of a feast but did not know where it would be held. "I wonder if Chameleon knows. Surely he must! I think I will go and see him," Spider mused.

With practiced art, Spider spun himself a silken silver thread. He lowered it to the ground and ran as fast as he could to where Chameleon lived.

"Good morning, Chameleon!" said Spider. "I hope you are well and have had a pleasant breakfast. You will be attending the feast, I presume?"

Slowly Chameleon swiveled his eyes in Spider's direction. "To which feast are you referring? I understand that there are to be several."

To Chameleon's surprise, Spider began to shake with excitement at the prospect of not one but several fine feasts.

"Which feast would you prefer to attend?" queried Spider casually, trying to pry more information out of Chameleon. But knowing of Spider's greed, Chameleon would not give away any clues.

"Oh, whichever one takes my fancy at the time," said Chameleon. "No doubt I shall see you there." And slowly he left, amused at Spider's discomfort.

Spider was very annoyed. He had not found out when or where any of the feasts were to be held. So he summoned four of his children and asked them if they knew the whereabouts of any of the feasts.

"Yes!" they all replied. "But we don't want to go to any of the feasts."

"Aha!" chuckled Spider. "You youngsters do not know how to enjoy life. You don't know how to look after yourselves. I always attend feasts!"

Spider gave each of his four children a thread and showed them how to tie the thread around their middles as he had done. As soon as they found a feast, they were to pull on their thread and Spider would follow the thread and so be able to attend the feast.

His children scuttled off in four different directions. Spider climbed into his favorite web and dozed off. Greedily, he dreamed of all the food he would eat. "Four feasts! Four beautiful feasts! And I shall attend them all as I am so clever!"

The next day, the first young spider came to Hare's home. Hare lived to the North and his feast was about to start. The young spider tugged excitedly at the silken thread around her waist and scurried to join the feast.

In the East, the second young spider found Leopard. The feast was about to start, so he tugged an urgent message on his thread and scampered to the meal.

The third young spider found Bullfrog in the West. He had started his feast. She also tugged her silken thread. In the South, the fourth young spider pulled at his silken thread too, as he dashed off to join Honey Badger's feast.

"Aha," gloated Spider, as he felt the tug of his first child's thread. He readied himself to join the feast to the North.

"Ooh!" cried Spider, as a second tug jerked him to the East. "Two feasts in

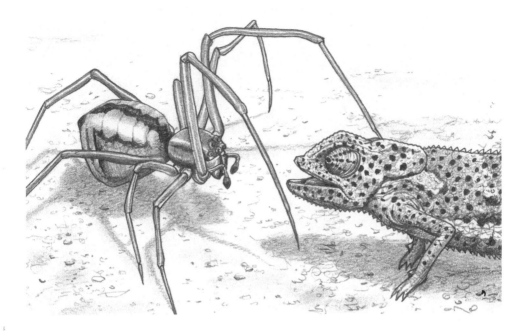

one day! Which should I attend?"

"Oh my," gasped Spider. This time he felt a strong pull to the West. "Whoever heard of three feasts in one day?" he exclaimed.

"Ow!" yelled Spider, as the fourth child pulled him to the South. "This is a disaster. Oh help! Help!"

All four children tugged and pulled their threads urgently and the threads tightened around Spider's waist. He could not decide which feast to attend. Leopard's would be a sumptuous affair, but Hare was closer, and Honey Badger served his favorites …

The threads were pulled tighter and tighter. Spider's waist became smaller and smaller. He had to make up his mind now, but the pressure of the threads was becoming unbearable.

Unable to decide, Spider became faint. Suddenly, all four threads broke. Spider was thrown onto his back, where he lay unconscious.

The sound of the drums rolled over the plains for a long, long time as the animals enjoyed their many feasts. All, that is, except greedy Spider. Chameleon's evasive answers had been Spider's undoing.

Spider's waist never recovered and, ever since, all spiders have had incredibly small waists. And spiders can no longer attend feasts as they can only eat very small amounts at one sitting. This is why they often bundle up their victims in their webs; so that they can eat them in their own time.

FACTS ABOUT CHAMELEONS
SPECIES:
AFRICAN FLAP-NECKED CHAMELEON
(*Chamaeleo dilepis*)
Solitary.

	Male	Female
Length	1 ft	1 ft
Weight	4 oz	4 oz
Length at Hatching	2⅓ in	2⅓ in
Age at Maturity	2 years	2 years
Incubation Period	—	150–300 days
Number of Eggs	—	25–40
Lifespan	5 years	5 years

Identification The African flap-necked chameleon is a large chameleon with a continuous crest of horny bumps on both its neck and back and its throat and belly. The tail is long and prehensile and the feet have opposing toes. Both of these features allow the chameleon to grip firmly. There are also prominent head flaps at the back of the head, which lie flat against the neck.

Color varies from pale yellow through green to shades of brown. The belly is white and the male has an orange throat patch.

The eyes bulge and can move and focus independently. The Shona people believe that Chameleon can look back into the past and see forward into the future at the same time.

Habitat Open woodlands, bush, and coastal forests.

Habits The African flap-necked chameleon spends much of its time in the trees stalking its food. They are solitary and very territorial. Chameleons have elaborate ritual fights when an intruder is discovered. This includes rapid color changes and head butting. When threatened, they inflate their flattened bodies, inflate the throat sac, raise their head flaps, and open the mouth wide, exposing the orange-red lining. They will also bite.

They are most active at night and turn blue-white in the dark, making them easier to find. Their main predators are tree snakes, monkeys, and some birds.

Diet The chameleon eats insects, particularly grasshoppers and beetles.

Breeding In spring, females will allow males to approach them. Courtship is brisk and mating may last an hour. The eggs develop within the female and she becomes very bloated. During this time she constructs a tunnel 10 inches (25 cm) long in damp soil and lays her eggs in the tunnel. This process may take up to 24 hours.

The eggs hatch 150 to 300 days later depending on the coldness of the winter. As with lizards, the young fend for themselves from birth.

Why Dung Beetle Is So Strong

(A Batonka story)

When you walk through the African bush during the rainy season, you may come across large black beetles pushing along large balls of animal dung as big as apples. These are known as Dung Beetles and this old Batonka story tells us why they do this.

Long ago, Dung Beetle and Butterfly were the best of friends. They were always together as they went about their daily business. One day, they were resting in the shade of a tree when First Man and First Woman walked by.

"Oh, what a beautiful butterfly!" they exclaimed. And they stood and admired her for quite some time.

When First Man and First Woman resumed their travels, Dung Beetle said to Butterfly, "Whenever First Man and his wife see you, they always stop and admire you. They never take a second glance at me. Am I so ugly?"

"Nonsense," said Butterfly. "It is only because you have nothing to attract their attention. Humans admire beauty and strength. If you were to become the strongest insect in the world, for instance, they would surely take notice of you."

"I could never become the strongest insect in the whole world!" said Dung Beetle sadly.

"Certainly you could," Butterfly quickly replied. "Remember, if you make no effort you can expect no results. But if you try you might succeed."

Dung Beetle decided that she would try. She went off on her own for a very long time. Dung Beetle tried all sorts of exercises and challenges to become strong. Through continued effort she became very strong. At last, she returned to her friend Butterfly.

To show Butterfly how strong she had become, Dung Beetle fashioned some huge balls of Elephant's dung. These balls were many times the size of Dung Beetle. But she was now so strong she had no trouble pushing them around with her back legs.

As Dung Beetle was doing this, First Man and First Woman passed by. They were both so amazed by Dung Beetle's prowess, that they did not even notice beautiful Butterfly.

Dung Beetle was pleased with all the attention paid to her and she has been pushing dung balls around ever since.

But Dung Beetle is not a vain creature, and she puts her feats of strength to practical use. She uses the dung balls to protect her eggs, which she buries inside the balls to give them extra protection from predators.

Dung Beetle's Burden

(A story from Ghana)

Long ago, Anansi, a cunning spider, and his son, Kweku Tsin, were very successful farmers. They grew fine harvests that were the envy of all their neighbors.

One year, however, the rains failed and it looked as though their seeds would not sprout. Kweku Tsin was walking through his fields when he met Chameleon. Chameleon asked why the young spider was so sad. Kweku Tsin told him that the crops would fail without rain.

Chameleon told Kweku Tsin to find two small sticks. He then told him to tap the sticks lightly on Chameleon's back in time to a magical song:

O water go up, O water go up
And let rain fall, and let rain fall.

To Kweku Tsin's joy it immediately began to rain. Kweku Tsin thanked Chameleon profusely and happily tended his fields. Within a couple of days, his fields promised to yield another fine crop.

Anansi soon heard how well Kweku Tsin's crops were growing. His own fields were bare and baked hard by the sun. Anansi demanded to know the secret of his son's good fortune. Kweku Tsin told his father about Chameleon's magic.

Anansi decided he would get his fields watered too. "My son made Chameleon water his fields with little sticks. I will make him give me twice the water with two big sticks!"

Anansi met Chameleon and told him of his problems. Again Chameleon

asked for two small sticks to be tapped on his back in time to his song. The cunning spider got the two large sticks he had concealed nearby and beat Chameleon so hard that he fell down dead.

The greedy spider was frightened, for he knew Chameleon was the Creator's favorite. He had to pass the blame for Chameleon's death onto someone else. Quickly, Anansi picked up Chameleon's limp, dead body and hid him high in the branches of a tall tree.

Not long after, Kweku Tsin came along to see if his father had any luck in getting rain for his crops.

"Did you see Chameleon, Father?" he asked.

"Oh yes!" replied Anansi. "But he has climbed up into this tree and I am waiting for him to come down."

"I will go up and fetch him," said Kweku Tsin, and he began to climb. He soon found Chameleon high in the branches but when he touched his limp body, Chameleon fell to the ground.

"Oh! What have you done, you wicked child?" cried Anansi.

"It doesn't matter," replied Kweku Tsin, who saw through Anansi's trick. "The Creator is very angry with Chameleon and promised a bag of gold to anyone who would kill him. I will go now and get the reward!"

"No!" screamed Anansi. "The reward is mine. I killed Chameleon. I will take his body to the Creator and claim my reward!"

The Creator was very angry with Anansi for killing Chameleon. He sealed Chameleon's body in a great round container and Anansi was made to push the ball around with him forever as a punishment. The only way Anansi could ever be rid of his burden was for another animal to offer to take it from him. Of course, no one was willing to do this.

After many years, Anansi was almost worn out by his heavy burden. One day, he met Dung Beetle.

"Will you hold this burden for me while I visit my son?" asked Anansi.

"I know your tricks, Anansi!" replied the Dung Beetle. "You just want to be rid of your burden!"

"Oh no, Dung Beetle," protested Anansi. "I will be back for it, I promise!"

Dung Beetle was very honest. He always kept his promises and so he believed Anansi. Dung Beetle braced himself against the huge ball and Anansi ran off. Needless to say, Anansi did not intend to keep his word. Dung Beetle waited in vain for the spider to return.

Although he was free of his burden, Anansi had to abandon his fields as he was scared of being found and punished further by the Creator. He had to live a life of fear and he was unable to grow his precious crops. Instead he had to hide all the time and set traps to catch food to eat.

Dung Beetle had to take over Anansi's burden. For the rest of his life he had to roll and push the large ball before him. This is why we so often see dung beetles pushing great balls as they move along.

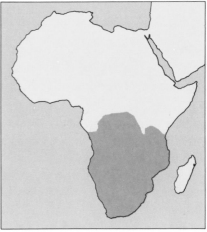

FACTS ABOUT DUNG BEETLES
SPECIES:
COMMON DUNG BEETLE
(Pachylomera femoralis)
Gregarious when feeding.

	Male	Female
Length	1 ¾ in	1 ¾ in
Weight	¾ oz	¾ oz
Larval Stage	2–3 weeks	2–3 weeks
Pupal Stage	Up to 1 year	Up to1 year
Incubation	1 week	1 week
Lifespan	2 years	2 years

Identification Dung beetles, or scarab beetles, are common throughout most of Africa and there are 750 known species. The common dung beetle is one of the larger members of the family. This large black beetle is easy to identify as the top of the wing case is flattened and dented, looking as though it has been crushed.

The middle and hind legs have well-developed, five-jointed feet, but the broad front legs end as if at the ankle.

These large insects fly strongly and are often seen zooming around the bush.

Habitat Found in most areas of sub-Saharan Africa, except for regions that are exceptionally dry and devoid of herbivores.

Habits These beetles have a very good sense of smell and are quick to detect fresh herbivore dung. Some smaller species make dung balls beneath the dry dung pile, whereas others make no balls at all.

The common dung beetle makes large tennis ball-size spheres of fresh dung, which are smoothed into shape by the strong, paddle-shaped front legs. The dung balls are then rolled away from the dung source even though they are many times the beetle's own size. This habit ensures that the dung ball is removed from the other common dung beetles and related species, as competition for fresh dung can be fierce. A large pile of elephant droppings can soon contain several hundred dung beetles, all working away feverishly.

Diet Dung beetles feed on fresh herbivore dung in wilderness areas and domestic livestock dung in farming areas.

Breeding The male makes a "nuptial ball," which he rolls away and uses to attract a female. He then buries the ball and he and the female stay in the hole for two or three days, mate and eat the ball.

When the "honeymoon" is over, the male or female prepares a "brood ball." This is also buried and the female lays a single oval, white egg ⅛ inch (3 mm) long in it. The nest is sealed up and the adults leave the nest to repeat the process elsewhere.

The egg hatches one week later and the white grub devours the inside of the ball. The outer surface of the dung ball hardens to prevent the food inside from drying out.

After two or three weeks, the grub forms a pupa and remains snugly concealed in the hollow dry shell where it changes into an adult beetle. This beetle will emerge with the next rainy season.

Dung beetle larvae are a favorite food of the mongoose and civet, who will spend hours searching for the nest holes and dig them up.

GLOSSARY

Acacia A family name for a common group of thorn trees widely distributed throughout the drier parts of Africa. The leaves are an important food for many animals. Many species of acacia tree also have nutritious seedpods—an important source of food in the dry season.

Afrikaans The language of the Afrikaner people, South African descendants of European settlers, particularly of Dutch origin.

Assegai A short, broad-bladed stabbing spear used by Zulu and Matabele warriors.

Browser An animal that eats mainly from trees and shrubs, taking leaves, twigs, and shoots.

Bush A general term applied to areas in southern Africa that still resemble their natural or original state.

Calabash *See* Gourd.

Camouflage The coloration or pattern of an animal that allows it to disguise itself against the background.

Carnivore An animal that lives by eating other animals. (*See also* Herbivore and Omnivore.)

Carrion The flesh of dead and sometimes rotting animals.

Diurnal A term describing an animal that is active during the hours of daylight. (*See also* Nocturnal.)

Ecology The study of the relationship between living things and their environment.

Endangered A term applied to an animal that is threatened with extinction, usually due to pressure from humans, either directly (from over-hunting and poaching), or indirectly (by removing the creature's habitat).

Environment The physical conditions and circumstances surrounding any living creature or plant that influences its existence and well-being.

Extinction   When a species no longer exists either in the wild or in captivity it is said to be extinct. Extinction is forever!

Forage   The activity of grazers and browsers searching for their food.

Gourd   The dried and hollowed-out shell of a fruit related to the melon. In Africa, gourds are widely used as water containers and drinking vessels. (Also known as a calabash.)

Grazer   An animal that feeds on grass.

Gregarious   Sociable. A gregarious animal is one that lives in herds or flocks.

Habitat   The place where a creature or plant naturally or normally lives.

Herbivore   An animal that eats only plants. (*See also* Carnivore and Omnivore.)

Hunter-gatherer   A term applied to nomadic tribes such as the Bushman of southern Africa, who live off the land rather than relying on crops and livestock.

Kopje   An Afrikaans name used throughout southern Africa to describe a small rocky hill or outcrop.

Kraal   An area surrounded by a stockade or fence, either for protecting livestock or a village.

Leguaan   A large lizard growing up to 6¾ ft (2m) long, common throughout most of Africa and closely associated with rivers and dams. (Also known as a water-monitor.)

Mammals   Animals that are warm-blooded, have milk-producing glands, have hair, and normally bear their young alive. This group includes humans, elephants, baboons, and bats.

Migrate   To move from one area to another. Many animals undertake seasonal migrations, often covering long distances, because of variations in food or water supplies due to changing seasons.

Muti   A southern African term for traditional tribal medicines.

Nganga	A southern African name for a person who knows about traditional tribal medicines and magic.
Nocturnal	A term describing an animal that is active at night. (*See also* Diurnal.)
Omnivore	A creature that eats both meat and plants. (*See also* Carnivore and Herbivore.)
Pan	A natural waterhole.
Predator	An animal that catches other animals for food.
Prehensile	A term describing something that is able to grasp by folding or wrapping around an object. Some monkeys have prehensile tails.
Prey	An animal caught by a predator.
Qunube tree	The qunube tree grows in southern Africa in areas of low altitude on the fringes of rainforests close to rivers, often on termite mounds. It varies in height from a shrubby growth to a well-shaped tree of 23 to 65 feet (7 to 20 m). The yellowish fruit is edible. (Also known as a bird plum tree.)
Reptile	A cold-blooded animal with scaly skin. Snakes, lizards, and turtles are reptiles.
Resource	Something available as a stock or reserve that can be used when needed.
Sanctuary	A safe place, such as a national park, where animals are protected from hunters.
Savanna	Large areas of natural grassland with scattered tree growth.
Scavenger	An animal that lives off the dead remains of other animals or plants. Jackals and vultures scavenge from the remains of lion kills.
Solitary	A term describing an animal that lives alone most of the time.

Species   A group of animals or plants with common characteristics and which do not breed with others outside the group.

Territory   An area used by an animal for feeding and/or breeding, often defended against its own kind and sometimes against other species too.

Veld   An Afrikaans word meaning open country or grassland.

Vlei   An Afrikaans name widely used in southern Africa for an area of marshy ground.

Wallow   A mud- or dust-bath in which animals lie and roll to çool off and obtain protection from ticks and lice.

Water-monitor   *See* Leguaan.

BIBLIOGRAPHY

AFRICAN INSECT LIFE. S.H. Skaife, C. Struik, 1976
AFRICAN MYTHS AND LEGENDS. Kathleen Arnot, Oxford University Press, 1962
AFRICAN MYTHOLOGY. G. Parrinder, Hamlyn Publishing Group, 1967
BANTU FOLKORE. Matthew L. Hewatt, M.D., T. Maskew Miller, 1906
BECHUANA FIRESIDE TALES. Phyllis Savory, Howard Timmins, 1965
BIRDS OF AFRICA VOL. 1. L. Brown, K. Newman, and E.K. Urban,
Academic Press, 1982
BIRDS OF AFRICA VOL. 2. E.K. Urban, C.H. Fry, and K. Newman,
Academic Press, 1982
BIRDS OF AFRICA VOL. 3. C.H. Fry, S. Ketch, and E.K. Urban,
Academic Press, 1982
COMPLETE BOOK OF SOUTHERN AFRICAN BIRDS. W.G. Illeron, P.J. Quinn, and
P.L.S. Hilstein, Struik Winchester, 1990
FIELD GUIDE TO THE LARGER MAMMALS OF AFRICA. Jean Dorst and Pierre
Dandelot, Collins, 2nd ed., 1972
FIELD GUIDE TO SNAKES AND OTHER REPTILES OF SOUTHERN AFRICA.
B. Branch, C. Struik, 2nd ed., 1990
FOLK TALES FROM ALL NATIONS. F.H. Lee, George C. Harrap & Co. Ltd., 1931
INSECTS OF SOUTHERN AFRICA. C.H. Scholtz and E.Holm, Butterworth
Group, 1985
LEGENDARY AFRICA. Sue Fox, Everton Offset, 1977
MATABELE FIRESIDE TALES. Phyllis Savory, Howard Timmins, 1962
MAMMALS OF THE KRUGER AND OTHER NATIONAL PARKS. H. Kumpf;
a publication of the National Parks Board of Trustees of the Republic of
South Africa, 1979
MAMMALS OF SOUTH AFRICA. A. Roberts, Mammals of South Africa
Trust Fund, 1954
MYTHS AND LEGENDS OF AFRICA. M. Carey, Hamlyn Publishing Group, 1970
OS ESCARABIDES DE AFRICA (SUL DO SAARA). M.C. Ferreira, Instituto de
Invetigacao Cientifica de Mocambique, 1962
ROBERTS BIRDS OF SOUTHERN AFRICA. G.L. Maclean, John Voekker Bird Book
Fund, 5th ed., 1985
SIGNS OF THE WILD. Clive Walker, Natural History Publication, 1981
SOUTH AFRICAN FOLK TALES. James A. Honey, M.D., Baker & Taylor, 1960
SPECIMENS OF BUSHMEN FOLKLORE. W.H.I. Bleek and L.C. Lloyd,
C. Struik, 1968
SWAZI FIRESIDE TALES. Phyllis Savory, Howard Timmins, 1973
TREES OF SOUTHERN AFRICA. K. Coates Palgrave, Struik Publishers, 2nd ed., 1983
THE MAMMALS OF SOUTHERN AFRICAN SUBREGION. Reay H.N. Smithers,
University of Pretoria, 1983
WHEN HIPPO WAS HAIRY. Nick Greaves, Trade Winds Press, 1988
WHERE THE LEOPARD PASSES. G. Elliot, Routledge & Keegan, 1949
WILD MAMMALS/BUNDU SERIES. D. Kenmuir and R. Williams, Longman
Press, 1975

FURTHER READING

AFRICAN TALES: FOLKLORE OF THE CENTRAL AFRICAN REPUBLIC. Polly Strong, Tell Publications, 1992
ANIMALS OF THE AFRICAN YEAR: THE ECOLOGY OF EAST AFRICA. Jane Burton, Holt, Rinehart & Winston, 1972
THE BLACK CLOTH: A COLLECTION OF AFRICAN FOLKTALES. Bernard Binlin Dadie, University of Massachusetts Press, 1987
VANISHING HERDS. Harshad Patel, Stein and Day, 1973
WHEN HIPPO WAS HAIRY AND OTHER TALES FROM AFRICA. Nick Greaves, Barron's Educational Series, 1988